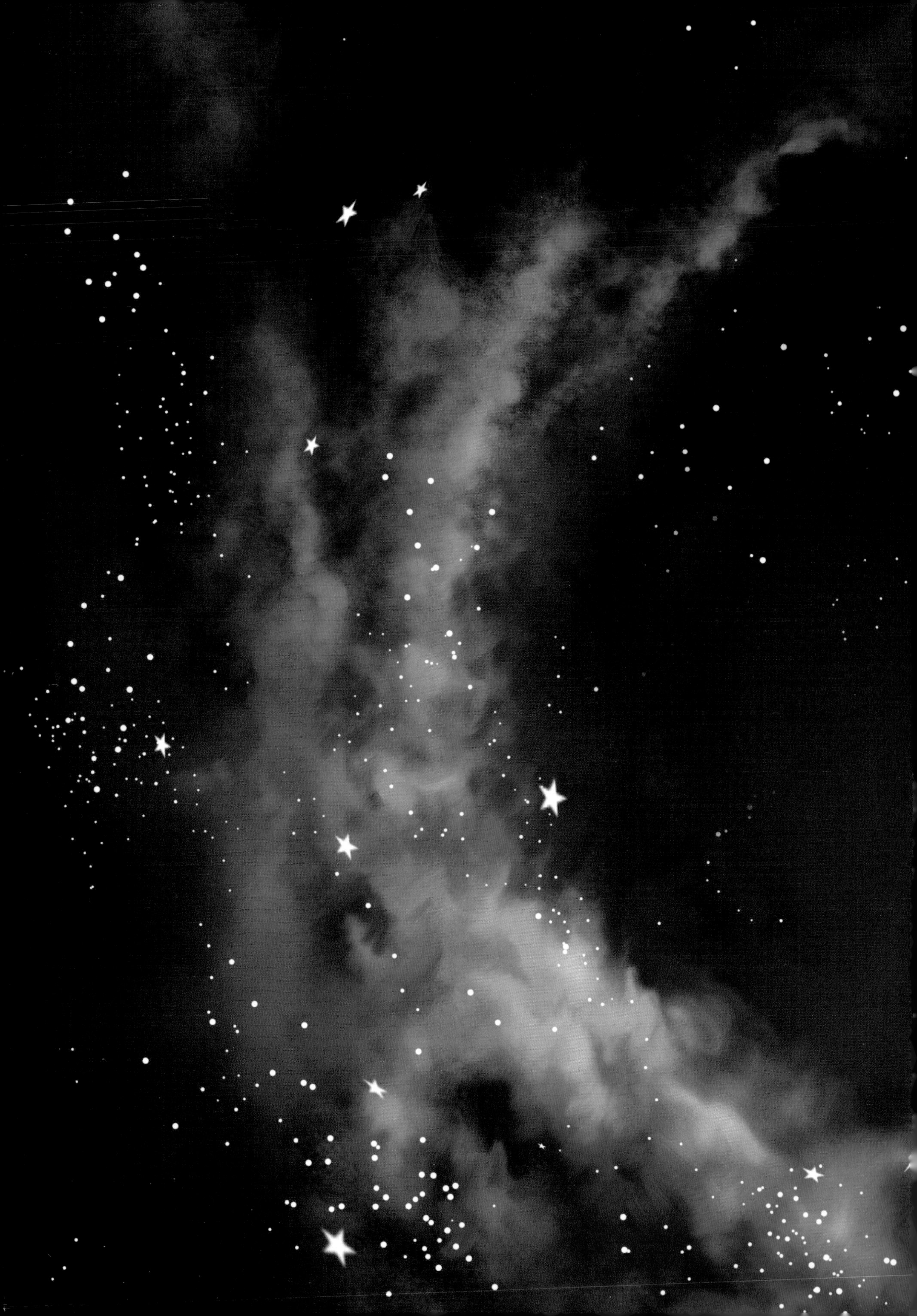

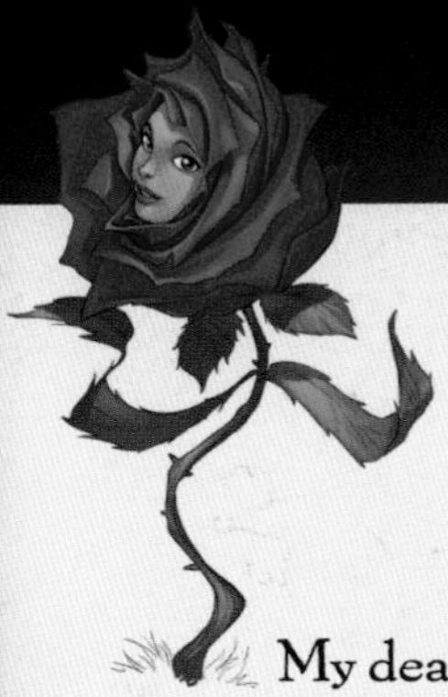

My dear Rose,

After leaving the planet of the Tortoise Driver, I treasure our correspondence even more, not just so I can tell you my adventures, but so I can find out how you're doing.

The Snake tried once again to keep people from communicating, and Fox and I were hard-pressed to stop him!

Our journey leads us to all sorts of planets, and whatever their differences may be, we have found that almost all their problems are due to a lack of communication, whether because of hostility or fear! And when people stop communicating, it's not just individual relationships that suffer, but the whole society starts to collapse.

The Little Prince

First American edition published in 2013 by Graphic Universe™.

Le Petit Prince ™

based on the masterpiece by Antoine de Saint-Exupéry

© 2013 LPPM
An animated series based on the novel *Le Petit Prince* by Antoine de Saint-Exupéry
Developed for television by Matthieu Delaporte, Alexandre de la Patellière, and Bertrand Gatignol
Directed by Pierre-Alain Chartier

© 2013 ÉDITIONS GLÉNAT
Copyright © 2013 by Lerner Publishing Group, Inc., for the current edition

Graphic Universe™ is a trademark of Lerner Publishing Group, Inc.

Graphic Universe™
A division of Lerner Publishing Group, Inc.
241 First Avenue North
Minneapolis, MN 55401 U.S.A.

Website address : www.lernerbooks.com

Library of Congress Cataloging-in-Publication Data

Bruneau, Clotilde.
　[Planète du Géant. English]
　The planet of the Giant / story by Gilles Adrien and Alain Broders ; design and illustrations by Élyum Studio ; adapted by Clotilde Bruneau ; translation, Anne Collins Smith and Owen Smith. — 1st American ed.
　　p.　cm. — (The little prince ; #09)
　　ISBN 978—0—7613—8759—6 (lib. bdg. : alk. paper)
　　ISBN 978—1—4677—1652—9 (eBook)
　　1. Graphic novels. I. Smith, Anne Collins, translator. II. Smith, Owen (Owen M.), translator. III. Adrien, Gilles. IV. Broders, Alain. V. Saint-Exupéry, Antoine de, 1900—1944. Petit Prince. VI. Élyum Studio. VII. Petit Prince (Television program) VIII. Title.
　PZ7.7.B8Pl 2013
　741.5`944—dc23　　　　　　　　　　　　　　　　　　　　　　　　　2013000319

Manufactured in the United States of America
1 — DP — 7/15/13

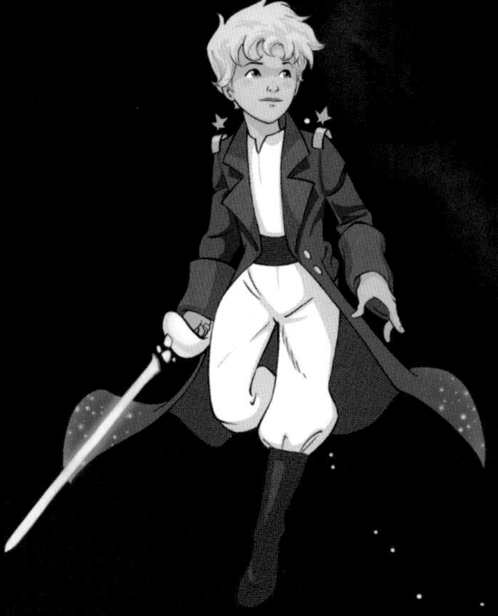

THE NEW ADVENTURES
BASED ON THE MASTERPIECE BY ANTOINE DE SAINT-EXUPÉRY

The Little Prince

THE PLANET OF THE GIANT

Based on the animated series and an original story by Gilles Adrien & Alain Broders

Design: Elyum Studio
Story: Clotilde Bruneau
Artistic Direction: Didier Poli
Art: Audrey Bussi
Backgrounds: Isa Python
Coloring: Karine Lambin
Editing: Didier Poli
Editorial Consultant: Didier Convard

Translation: Anne and Owen Smith

Graphic Universe™ • Minneapolis

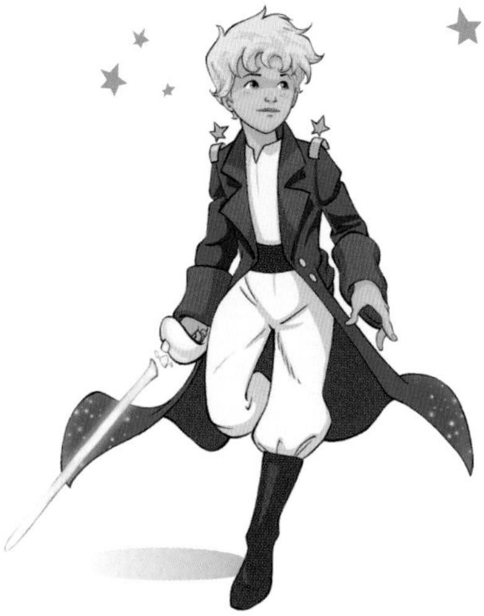

THE LITTLE PRINCE

The Little Prince has extraordinary gifts. His sense of wonder allows him to discover what no one else can see. The Little Prince can communicate with all the beings in the universe, even the animals and plants. His powers grow over the course of his adventures.

The Prince's uniform:
When he transforms into the uniform of a prince, he is more agile and quick. When faced with difficult situations, the Little Prince also uses a sword that lets him sketch and bring to life anything from his imagination.

His sketchbook:
When he is not in his Prince's clothing, the Little Prince carries a sketchbook. When he blows on the pages, they take wing and form objects that he'll find very useful. Like his sword, it's powered by stardust collected on his travels.

FOX

A grouch, a trickster, and, so he says, interested only in his next meal, Fox is in reality the Little Prince's best friend. As such, he is always there to give him help but also just as much to help him to grow and to learn about the world.

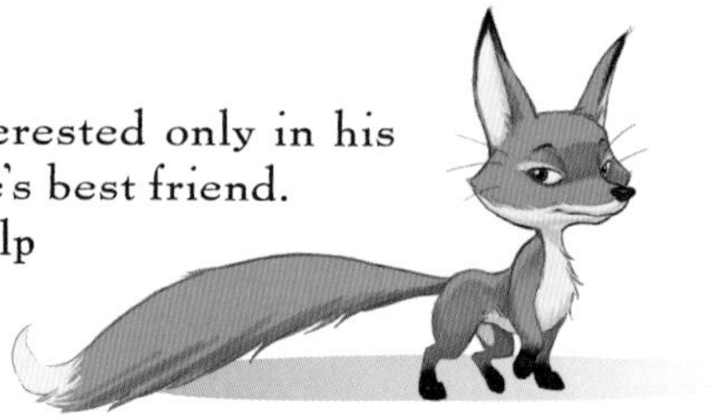

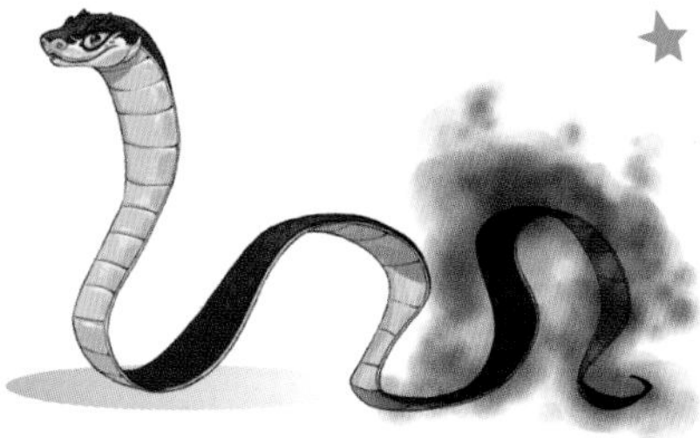

THE SNAKE

Even though the Little Prince still does not know exactly why, there can be no doubt that the Snake has set his mind to plunging the entire universe into darkness! And to accomplish his goal, this malicious being is ready to use any form of deception. However, the Snake never takes action himself. He prefers to bring out the wickedness in those beings he has chosen to bite, tempting them to put their own worlds in danger.

THE GLOOMIES

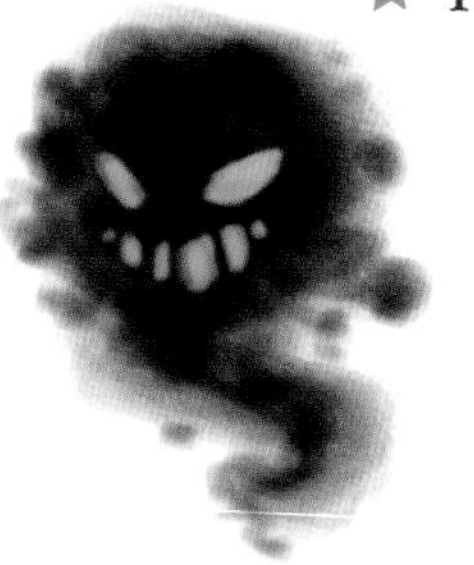

When people who have been "bitten" by the Snake have completely destroyed their own planets, they become Gloomies, slaves to their Snake master. The Gloomies act as a group and carry out the Snake's most vile orders so he can get the better of the Little Prince!

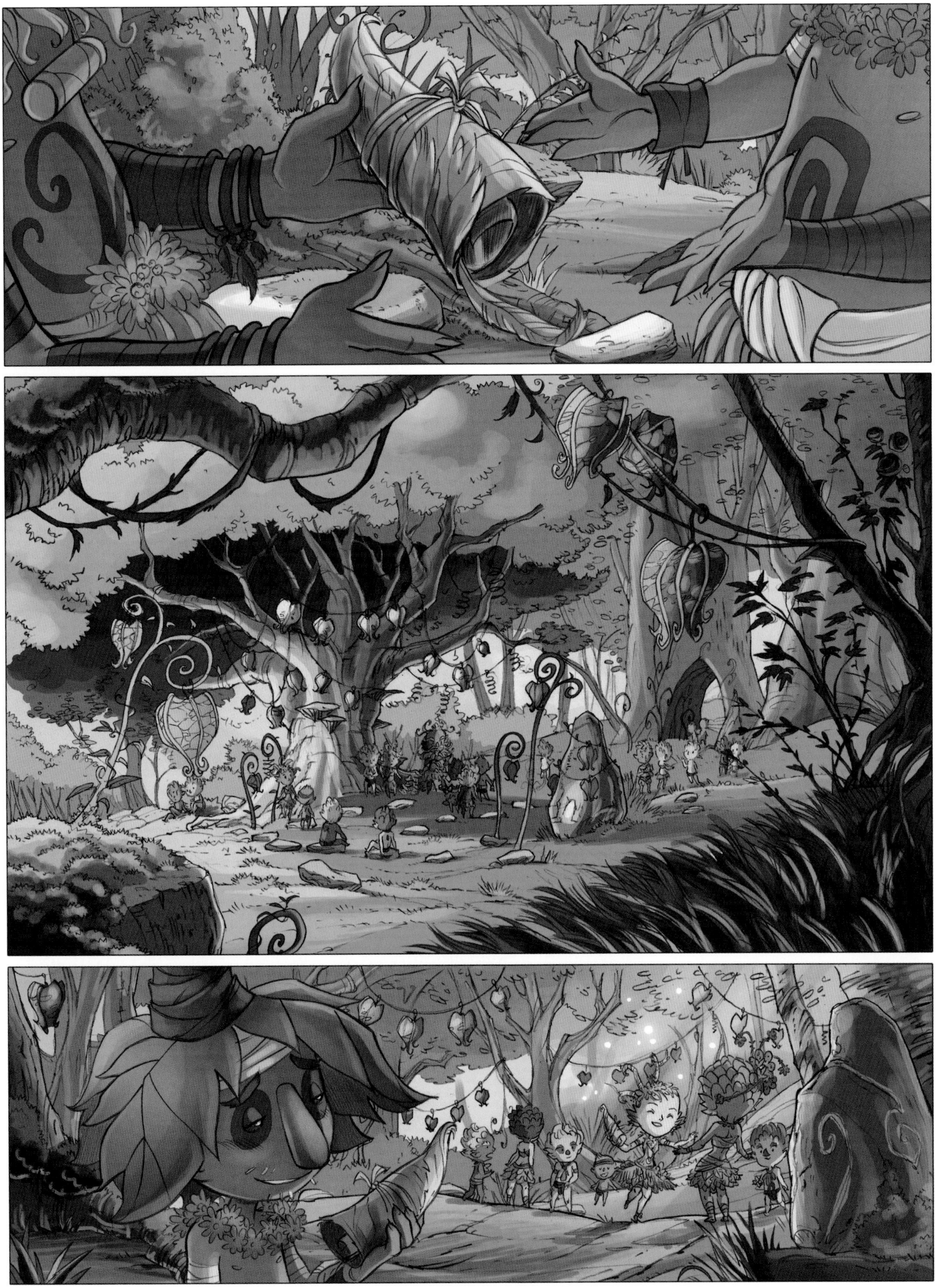

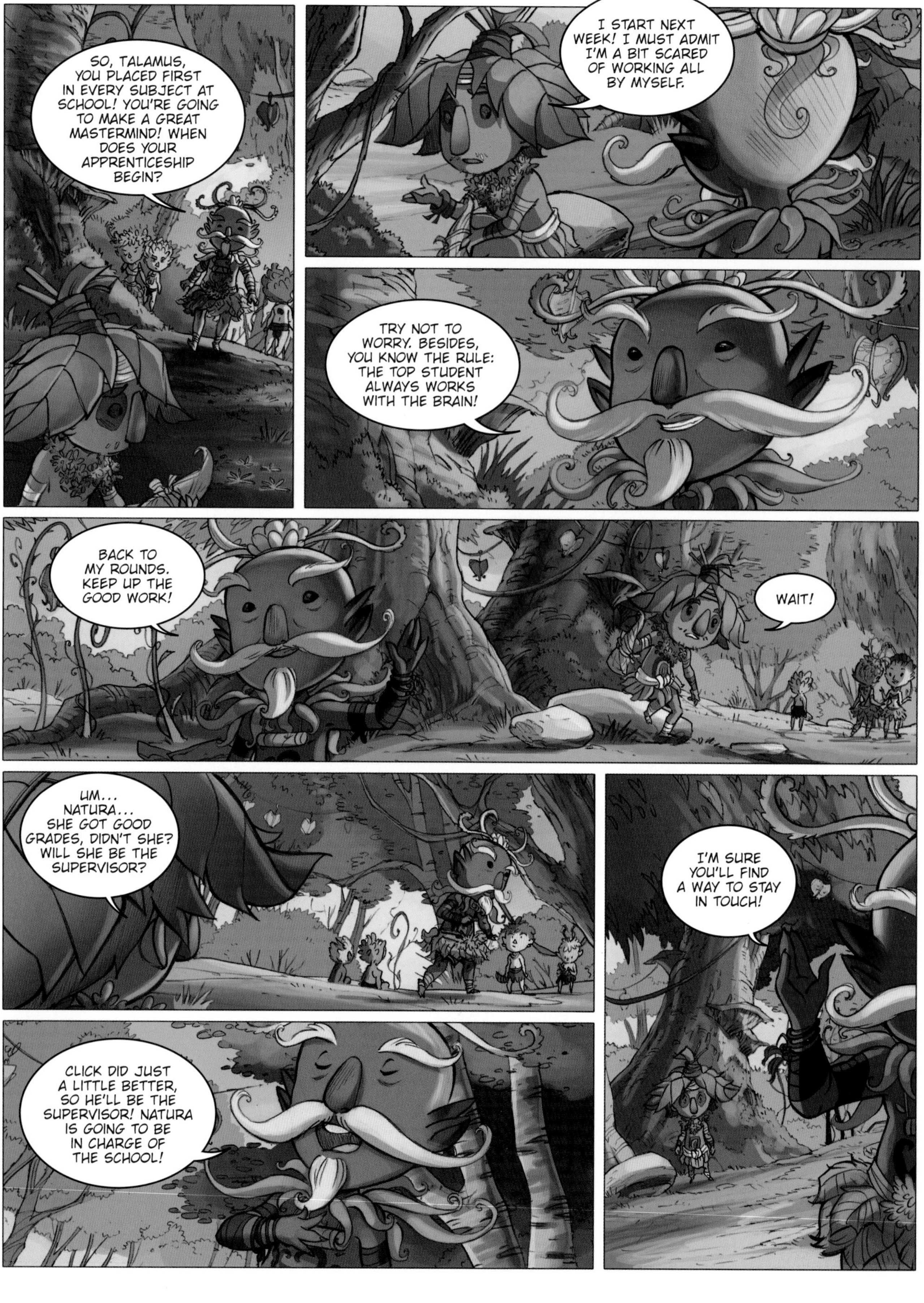
SO, TALAMUS, YOU PLACED FIRST IN EVERY SUBJECT AT SCHOOL! YOU'RE GOING TO MAKE A GREAT MASTERMIND! WHEN DOES YOUR APPRENTICESHIP BEGIN?
I START NEXT WEEK! I MUST ADMIT I'M A BIT SCARED OF WORKING ALL BY MYSELF.
TRY NOT TO WORRY. BESIDES, YOU KNOW THE RULE: THE TOP STUDENT ALWAYS WORKS WITH THE BRAIN!
BACK TO MY ROUNDS. KEEP UP THE GOOD WORK!
WAIT!
UM... NATURA... SHE GOT GOOD GRADES, DIDN'T SHE? WILL SHE BE THE SUPERVISOR?
CLICK DID JUST A LITTLE BETTER, SO HE'LL BE THE SUPERVISOR! NATURA IS GOING TO BE IN CHARGE OF THE SCHOOL!
I'M SURE YOU'LL FIND A WAY TO STAY IN TOUCH!

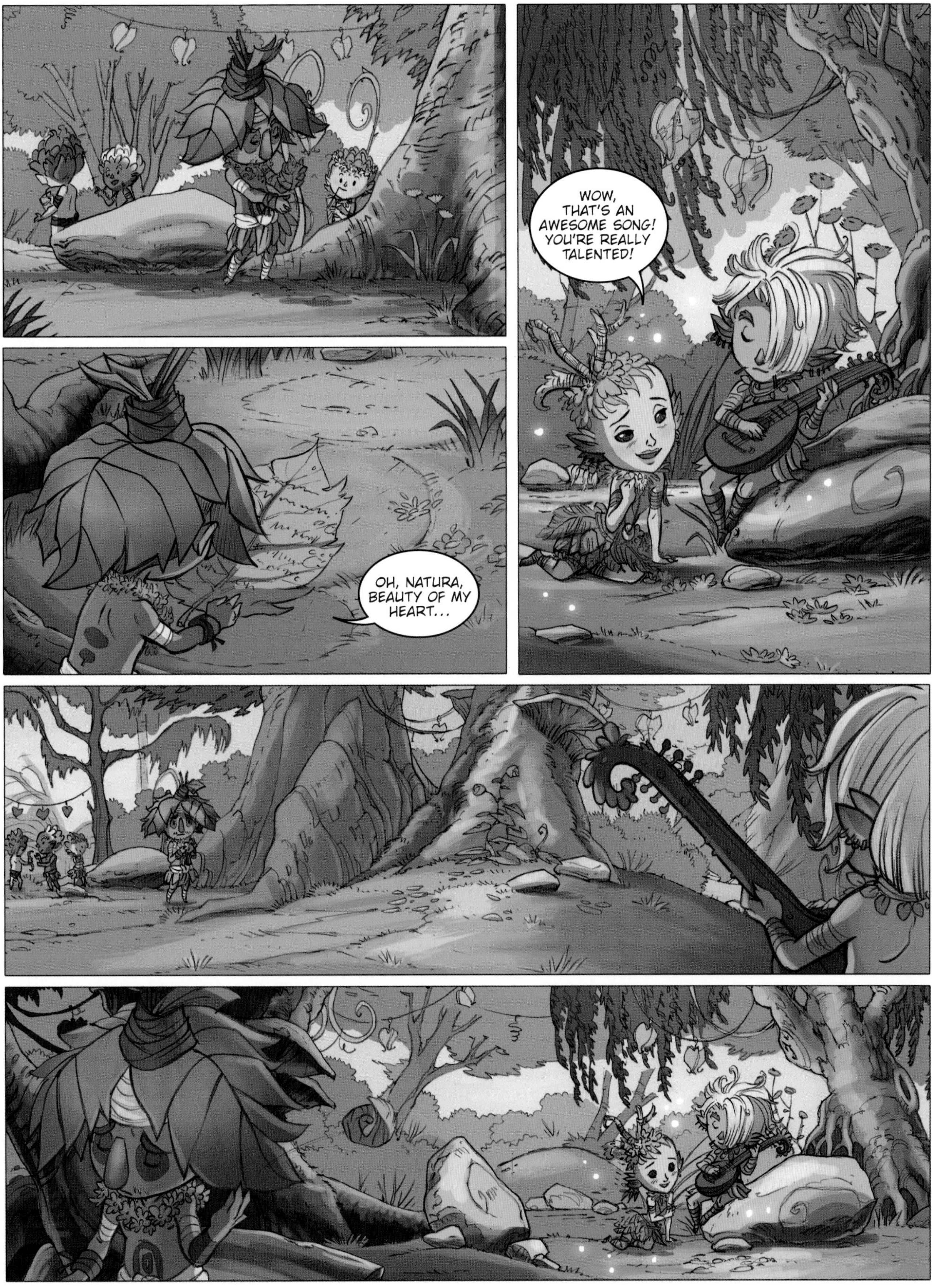
OH, NATURA, BEAUTY OF MY HEART...
WOW, THAT'S AN AWESOME SONG! YOU'RE REALLY TALENTED!

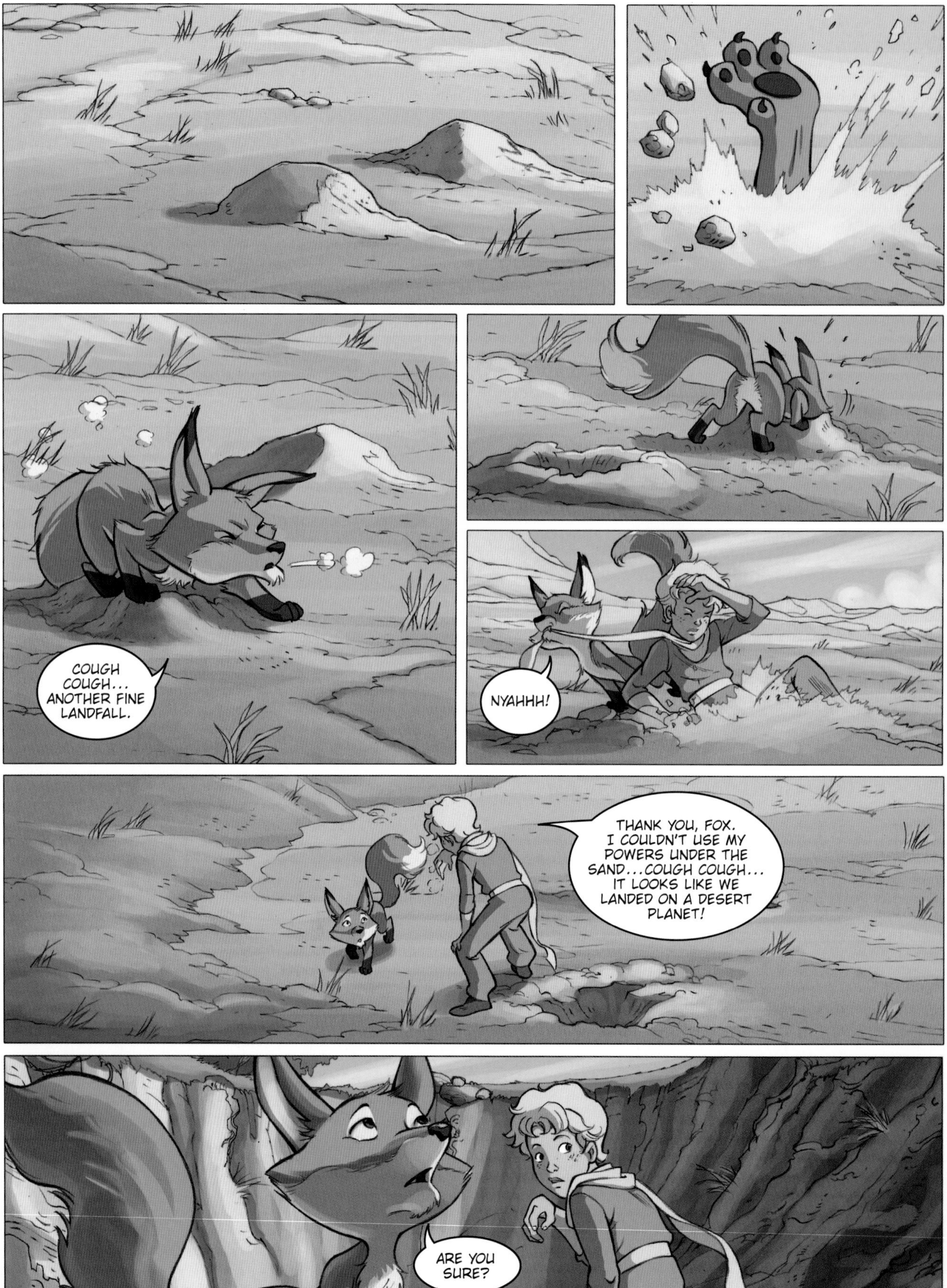
COUGH COUGH... ANOTHER FINE LANDFALL.
NYAHHH!
THANK YOU, FOX. I COULDN'T USE MY POWERS UNDER THE SAND...COUGH COUGH... IT LOOKS LIKE WE LANDED ON A DESERT PLANET!
ARE YOU SURE?

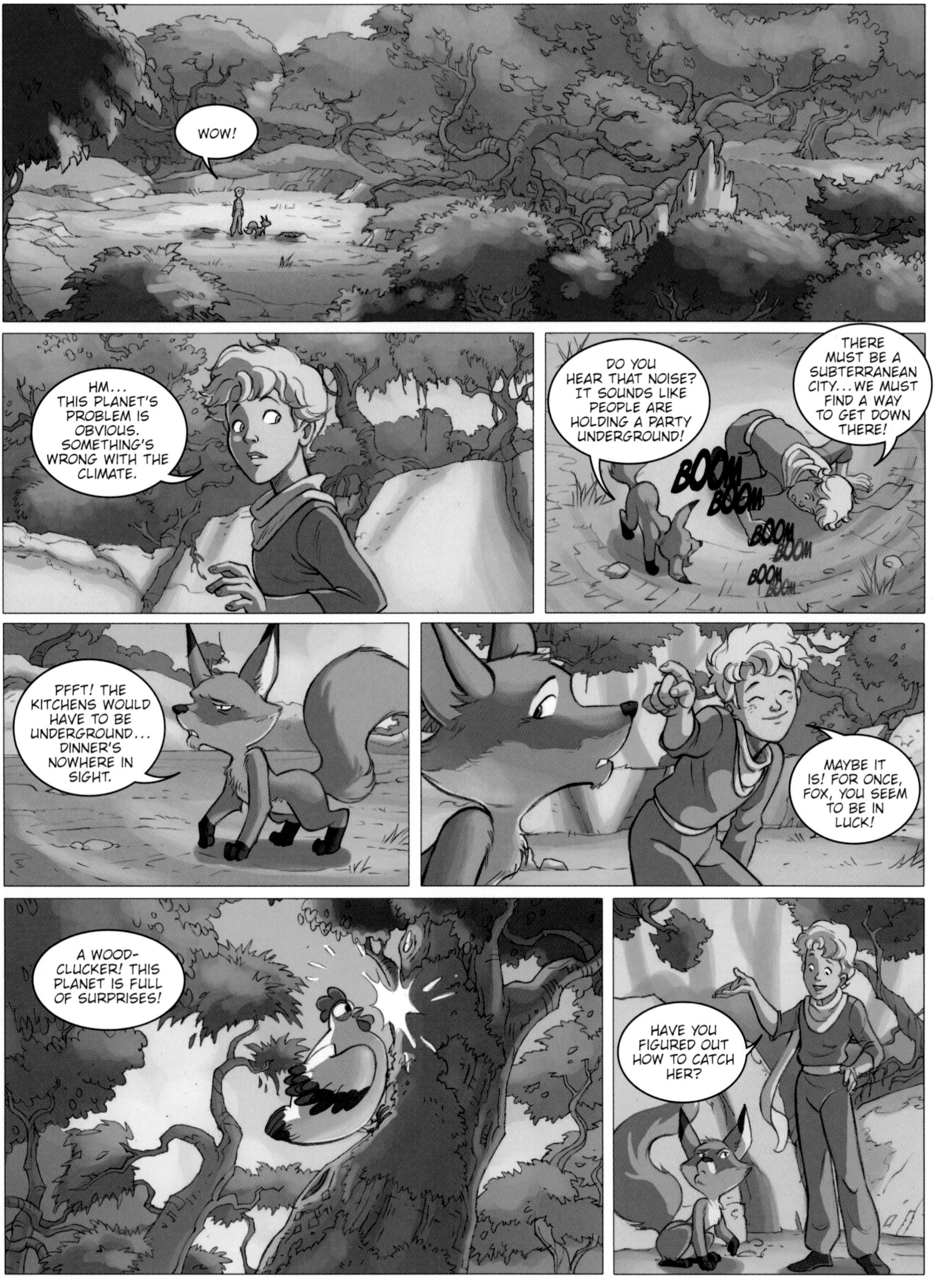
WOW!
HM... THIS PLANET'S PROBLEM IS OBVIOUS. SOMETHING'S WRONG WITH THE CLIMATE.
DO YOU HEAR THAT NOISE? IT SOUNDS LIKE PEOPLE ARE HOLDING A PARTY UNDERGROUND!
BOOM BOOM BOOM BOOM BOOM BOOM
THERE MUST BE A SUBTERRANEAN CITY... WE MUST FIND A WAY TO GET DOWN THERE!
PFFT! THE KITCHENS WOULD HAVE TO BE UNDERGROUND... DINNER'S NOWHERE IN SIGHT.
MAYBE IT IS! FOR ONCE, FOX, YOU SEEM TO BE IN LUCK!
A WOOD-CLUCKER! THIS PLANET IS FULL OF SURPRISES!
HAVE YOU FIGURED OUT HOW TO CATCH HER?

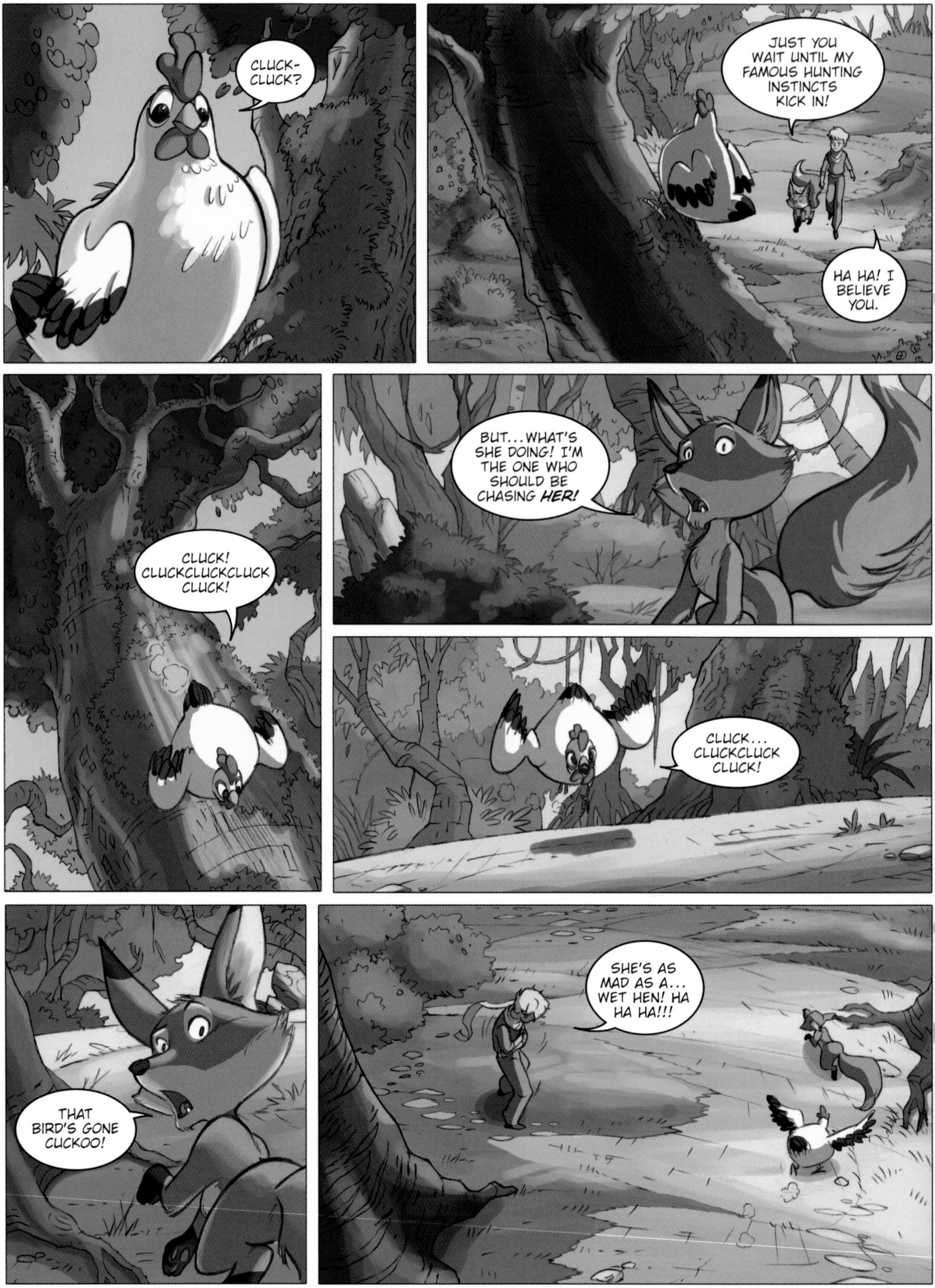
CLUCK-CLUCK?
JUST YOU WAIT UNTIL MY FAMOUS HUNTING INSTINCTS KICK IN!
HA HA! I BELIEVE YOU.
CLUCK! CLUCKCLUCKCLUCK CLUCK!
BUT...WHAT'S SHE DOING! I'M THE ONE WHO SHOULD BE CHASING HER!
CLUCK... CLUCKCLUCK CLUCK!
THAT BIRD'S GONE CUCKOO!
SHE'S AS MAD AS A... WET HEN! HA HA HA!!!

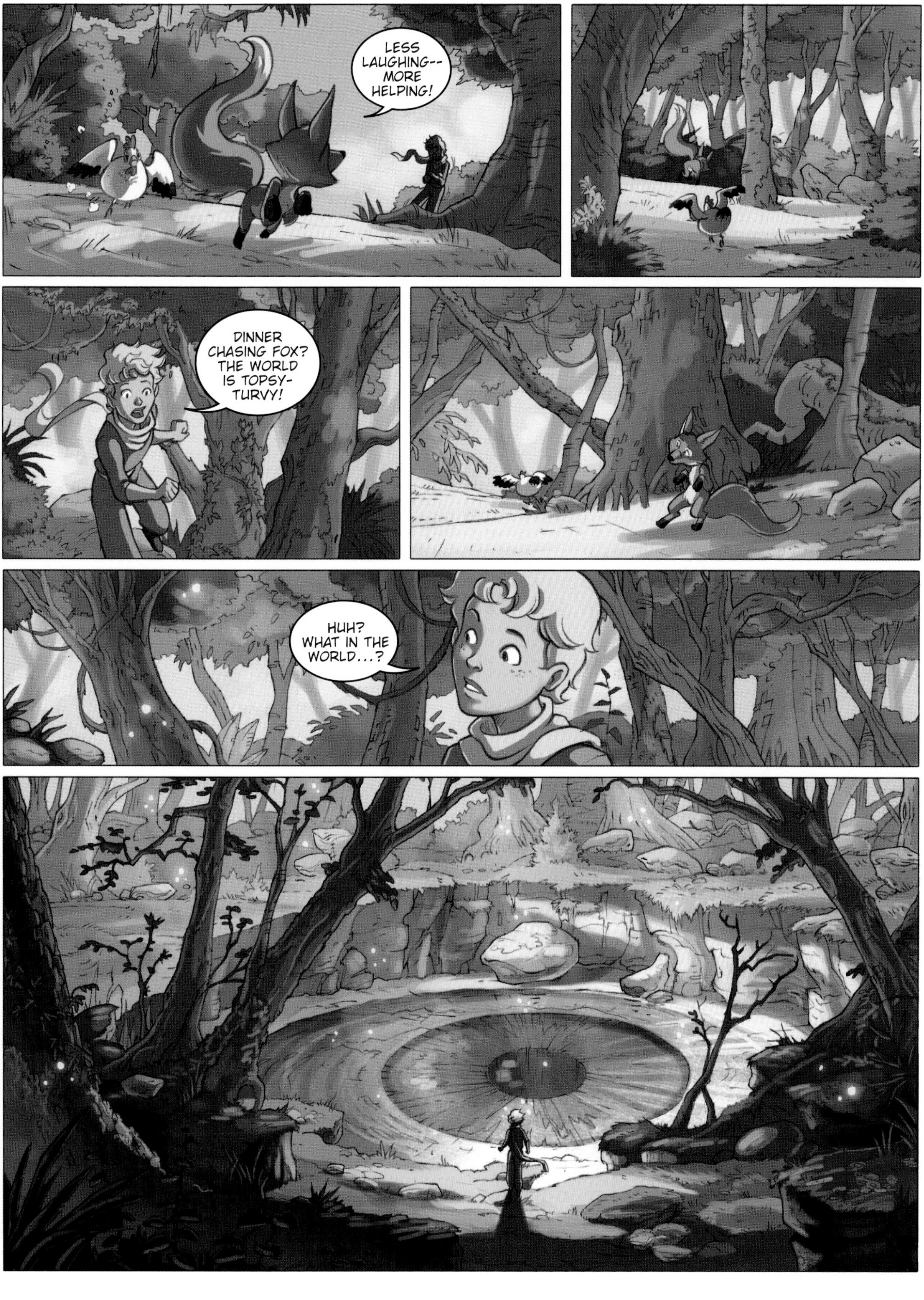
LESS LAUGHING-- MORE HELPING!
DINNER CHASING FOX? THE WORLD IS TOPSY-TURVY!
HUH? WHAT IN THE WORLD...?

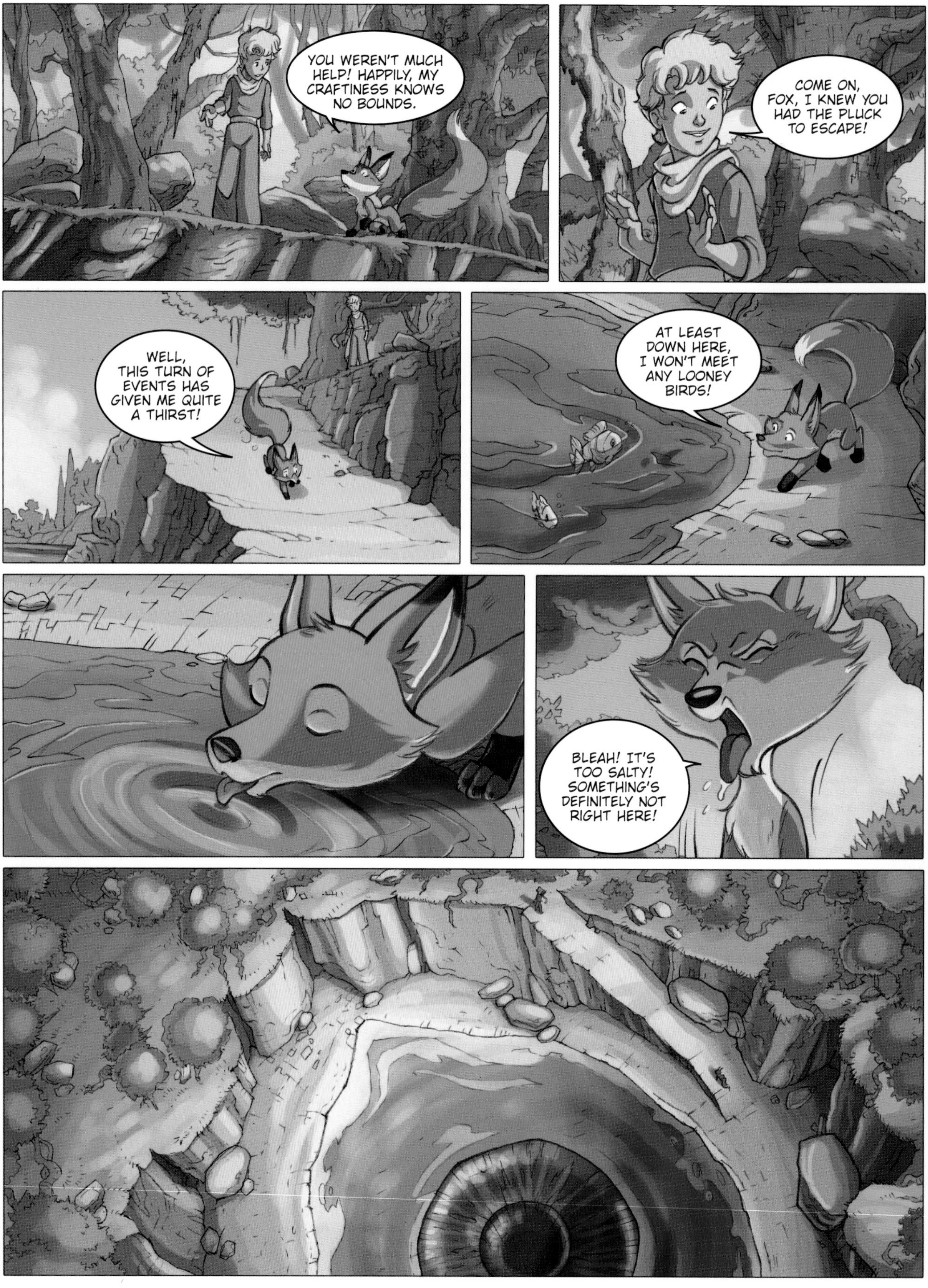
YOU WEREN'T MUCH HELP! HAPPILY, MY CRAFTINESS KNOWS NO BOUNDS.
COME ON, FOX, I KNEW YOU HAD THE PLUCK TO ESCAPE!
WELL, THIS TURN OF EVENTS HAS GIVEN ME QUITE A THIRST!
AT LEAST DOWN HERE, I WON'T MEET ANY LOONEY BIRDS!
BLEAH! IT'S TOO SALTY! SOMETHING'S DEFINITELY NOT RIGHT HERE!

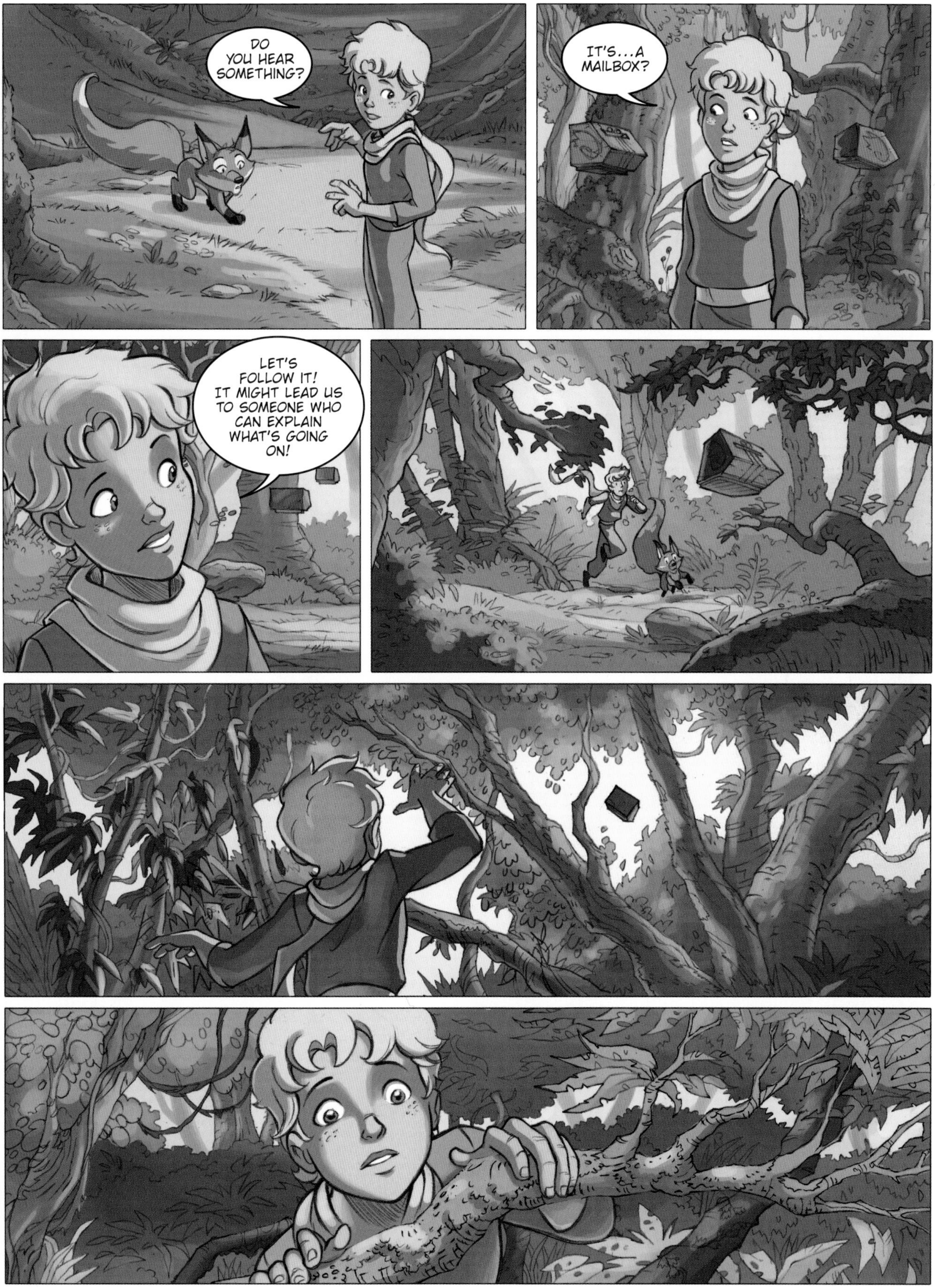
DO YOU HEAR SOMETHING?
IT'S...A MAILBOX?
LET'S FOLLOW IT! IT MIGHT LEAD US TO SOMEONE WHO CAN EXPLAIN WHAT'S GOING ON!

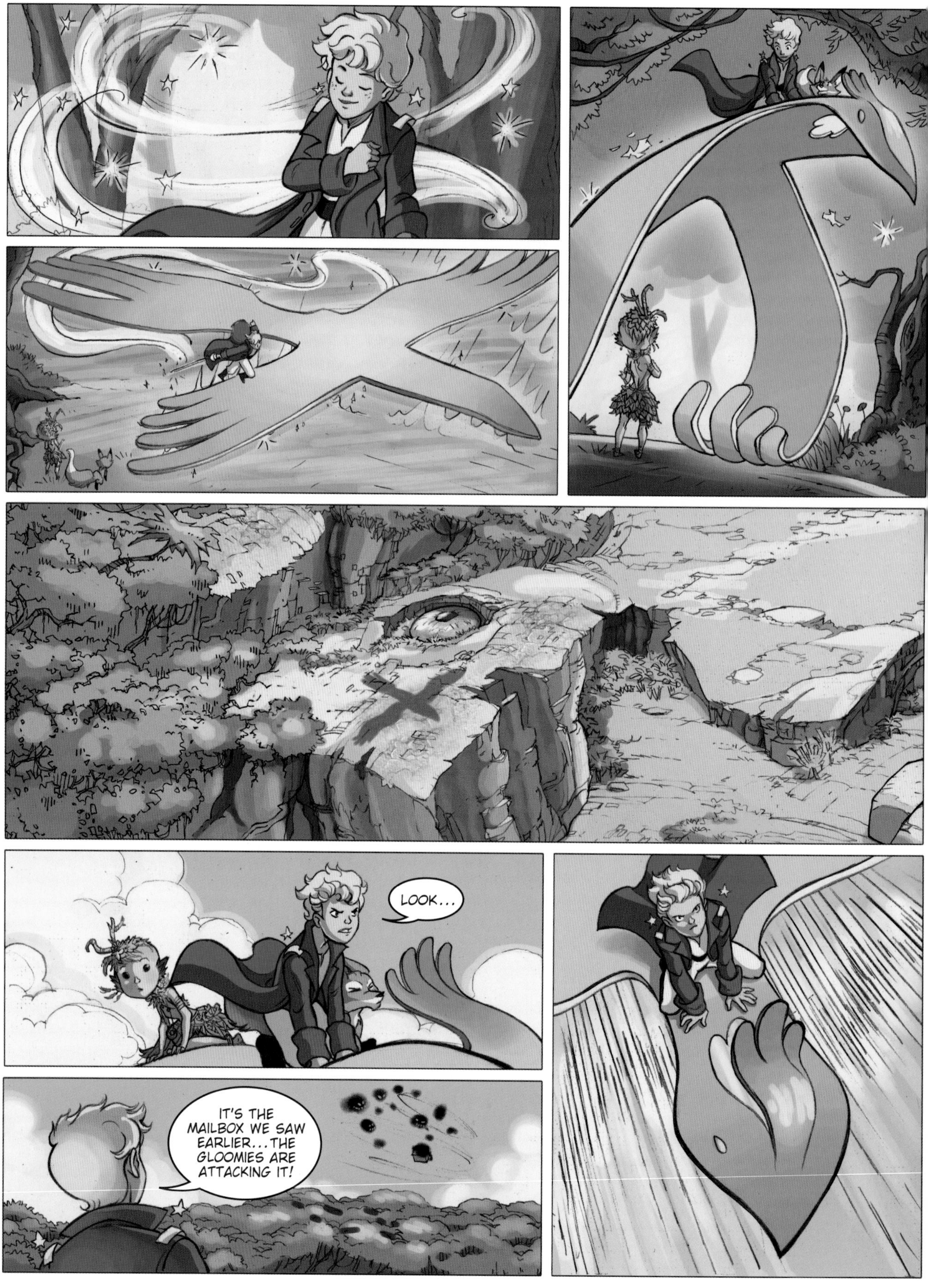
LOOK...
IT'S THE MAILBOX WE SAW EARLIER... THE GLOOMIES ARE ATTACKING IT!

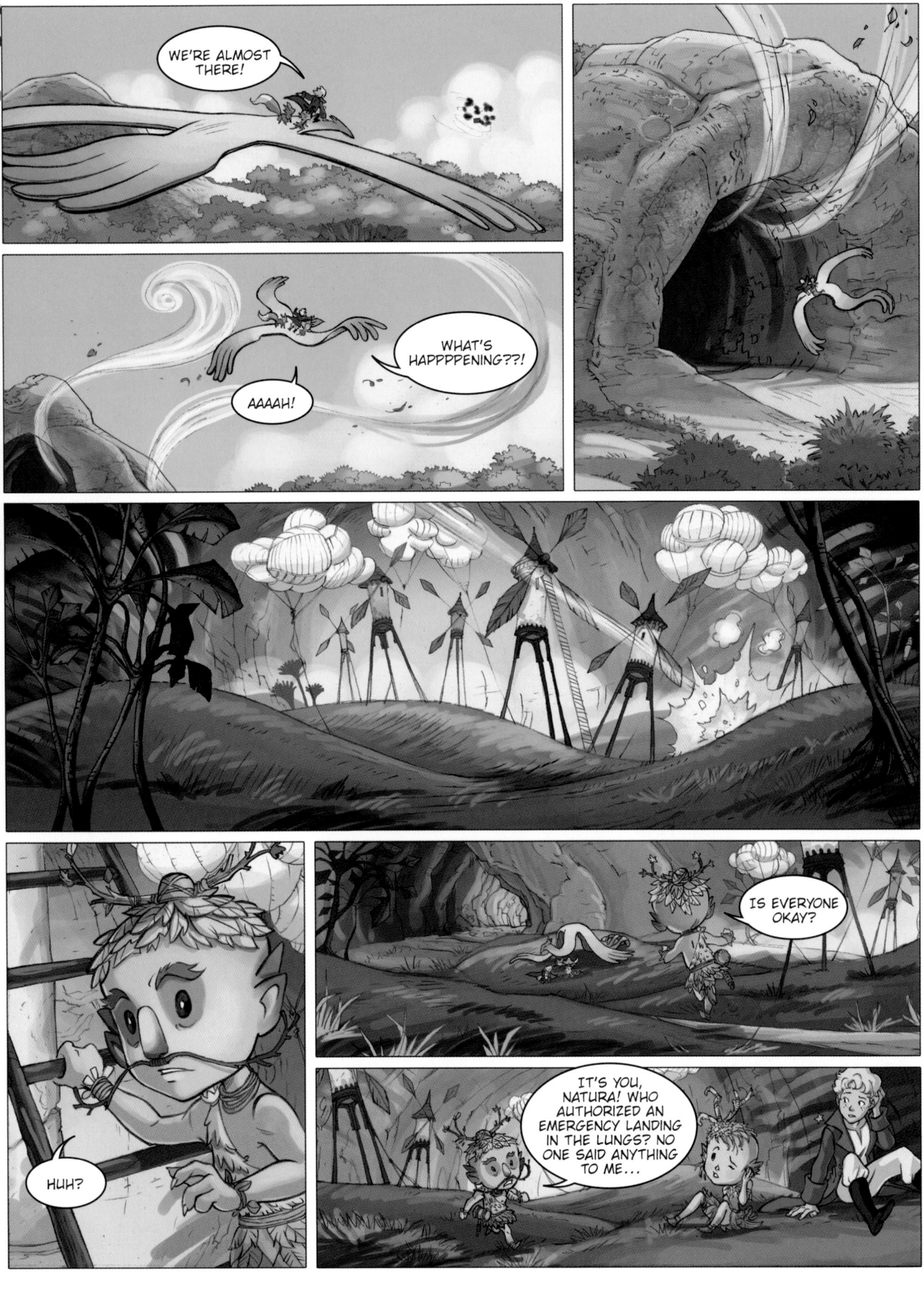
WE'RE ALMOST THERE!
WHAT'S HAPPPPENING??!
AAAAH!
IS EVERYONE OKAY?
HUH?
IT'S YOU, NATURA! WHO AUTHORIZED AN EMERGENCY LANDING IN THE LUNGS? NO ONE SAID ANYTHING TO ME...

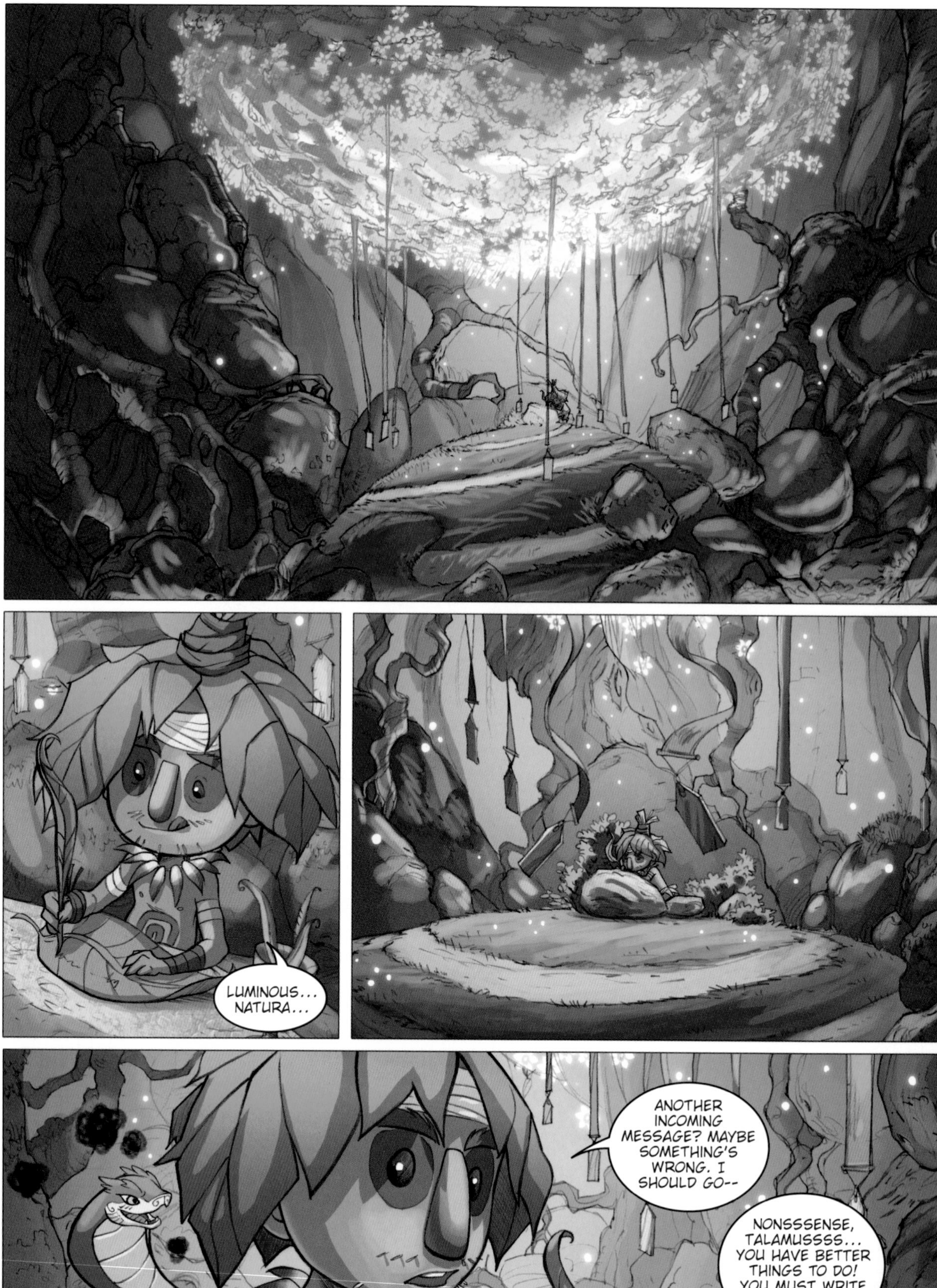
LUMINOUS... NATURA...
ANOTHER INCOMING MESSAGE? MAYBE SOMETHING'S WRONG. I SHOULD GO--
NONSSSENSE, TALAMUSSSS... YOU HAVE BETTER THINGS TO DO! YOU MUST WRITE YOUR POEMS... HSS...

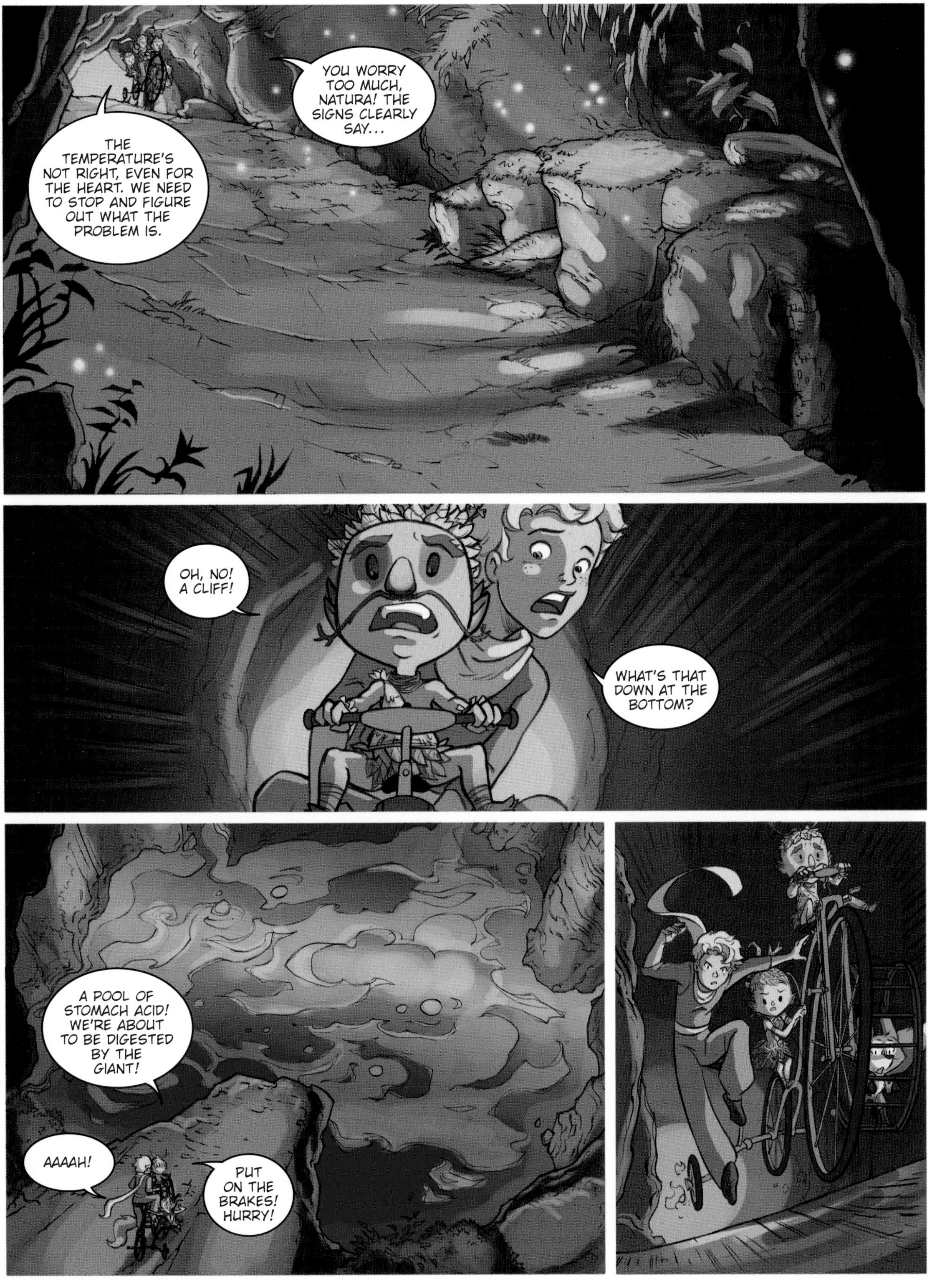
THE TEMPERATURE'S NOT RIGHT, EVEN FOR THE HEART. WE NEED TO STOP AND FIGURE OUT WHAT THE PROBLEM IS.
YOU WORRY TOO MUCH, NATURA! THE SIGNS CLEARLY SAY...
OH, NO! A CLIFF!
WHAT'S THAT DOWN AT THE BOTTOM?
A POOL OF STOMACH ACID! WE'RE ABOUT TO BE DIGESTED BY THE GIANT!
AAAAH!
PUT ON THE BRAKES! HURRY!

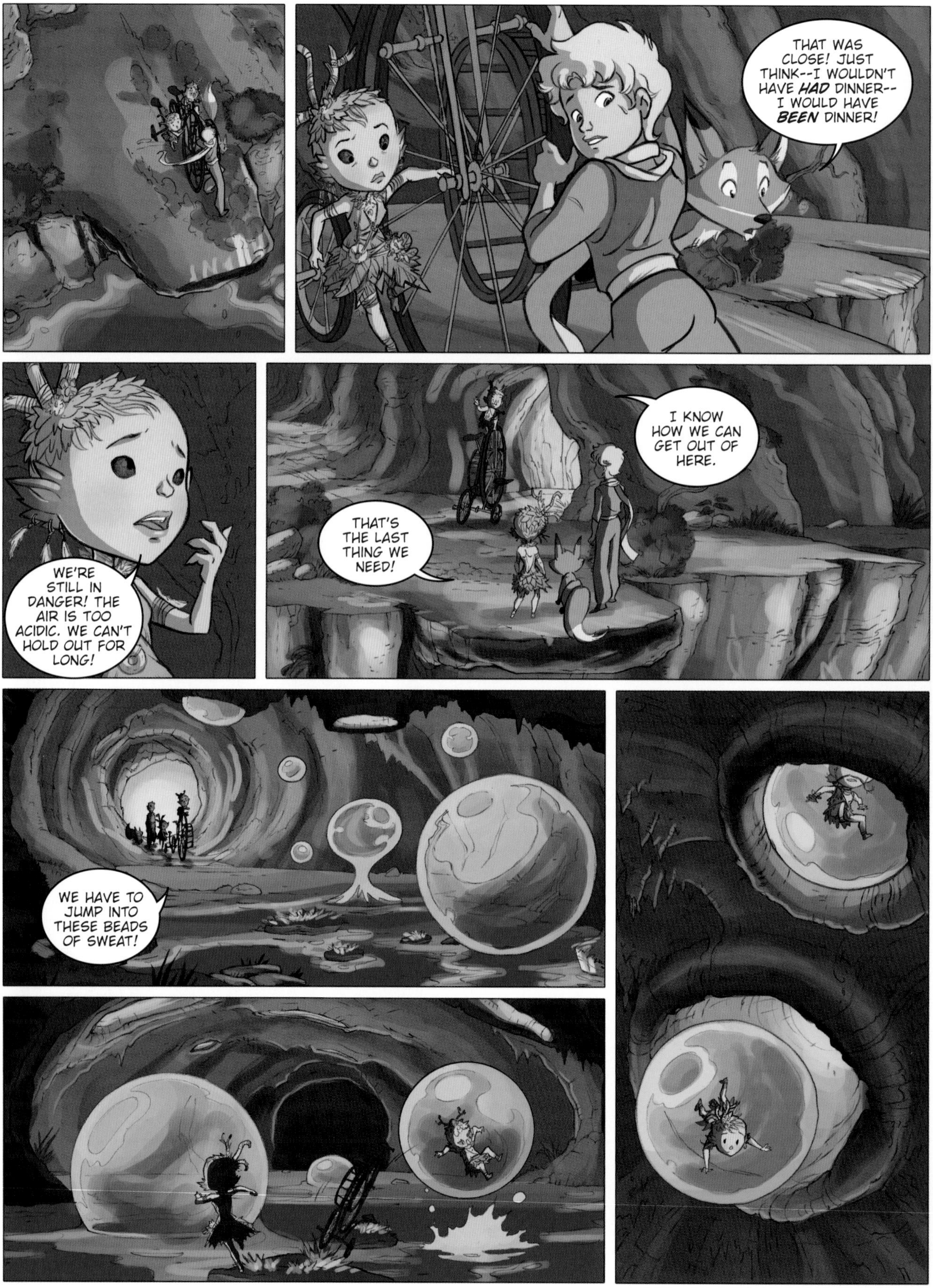
THAT WAS CLOSE! JUST THINK--I WOULDN'T HAVE *HAD* DINNER--I WOULD HAVE *BEEN* DINNER!
WE'RE STILL IN DANGER! THE AIR IS TOO ACIDIC. WE CAN'T HOLD OUT FOR LONG!
I KNOW HOW WE CAN GET OUT OF HERE.
THAT'S THE LAST THING WE NEED!
WE HAVE TO JUMP INTO THESE BEADS OF SWEAT!

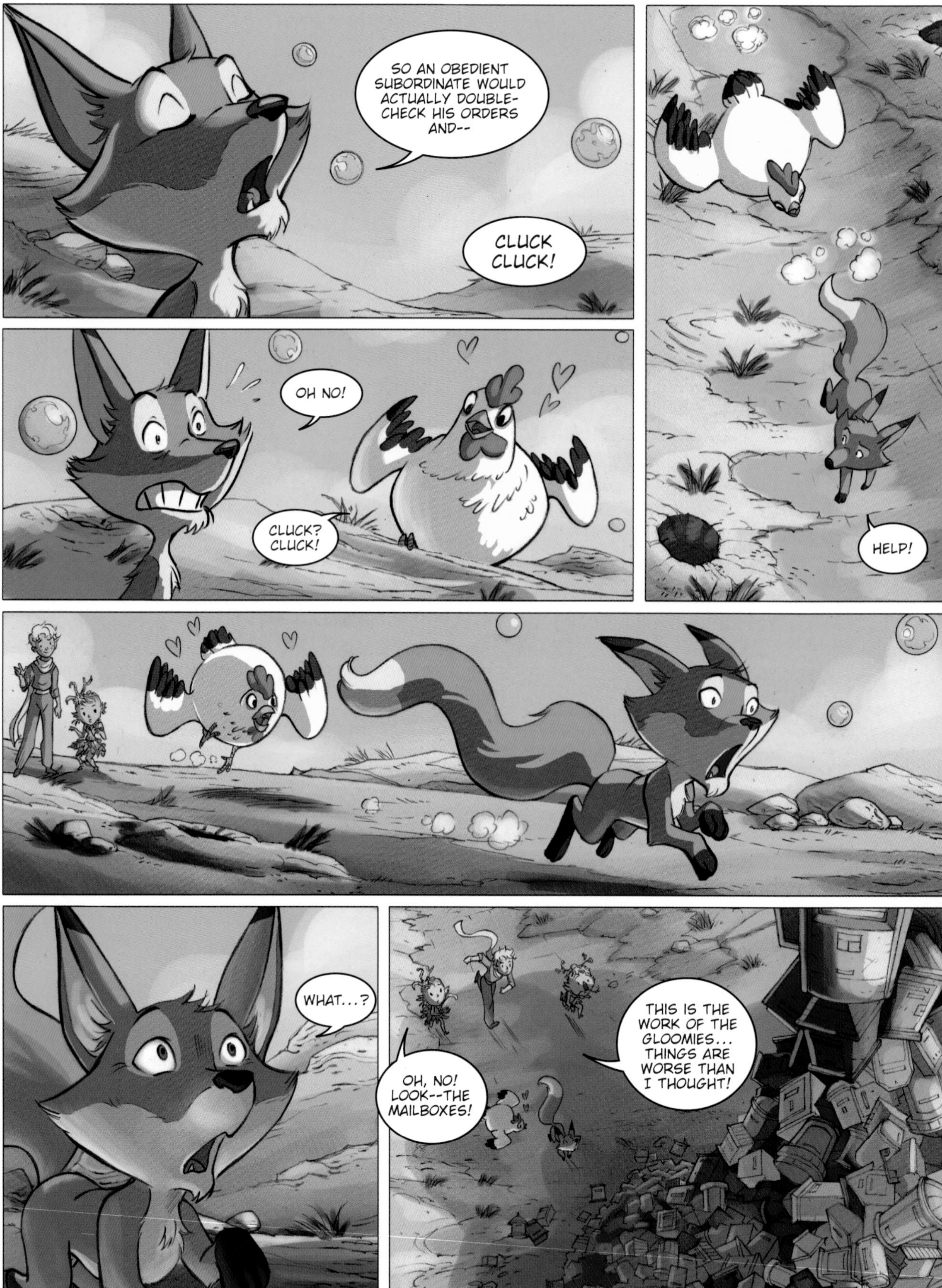
SO AN OBEDIENT SUBORDINATE WOULD ACTUALLY DOUBLE-CHECK HIS ORDERS AND--
CLUCK CLUCK!
OH NO!
CLUCK? CLUCK!
HELP!
WHAT...?
THIS IS THE WORK OF THE GLOOMIES... THINGS ARE WORSE THAN I THOUGHT!
OH, NO! LOOK--THE MAILBOXES!

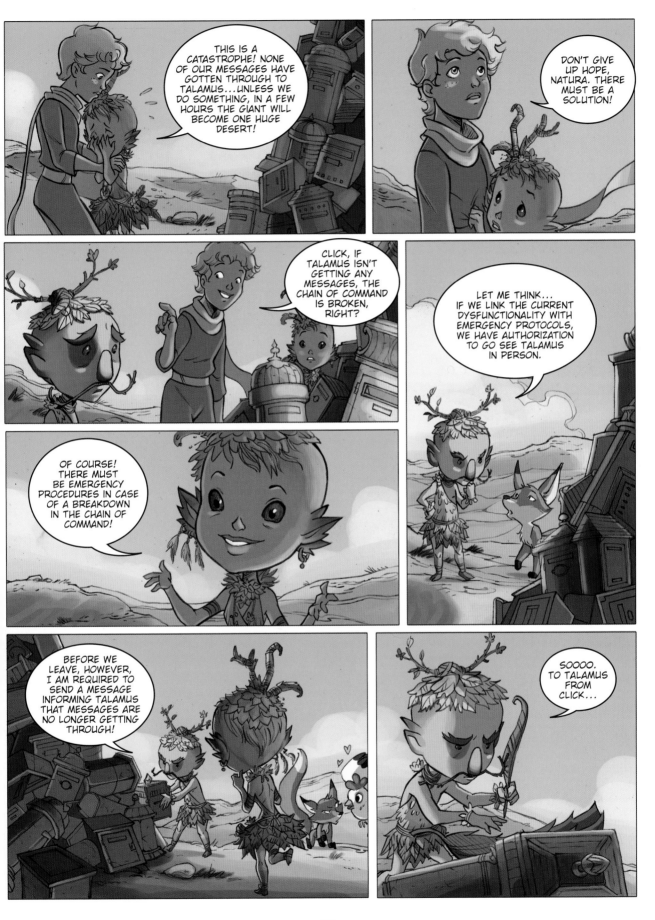

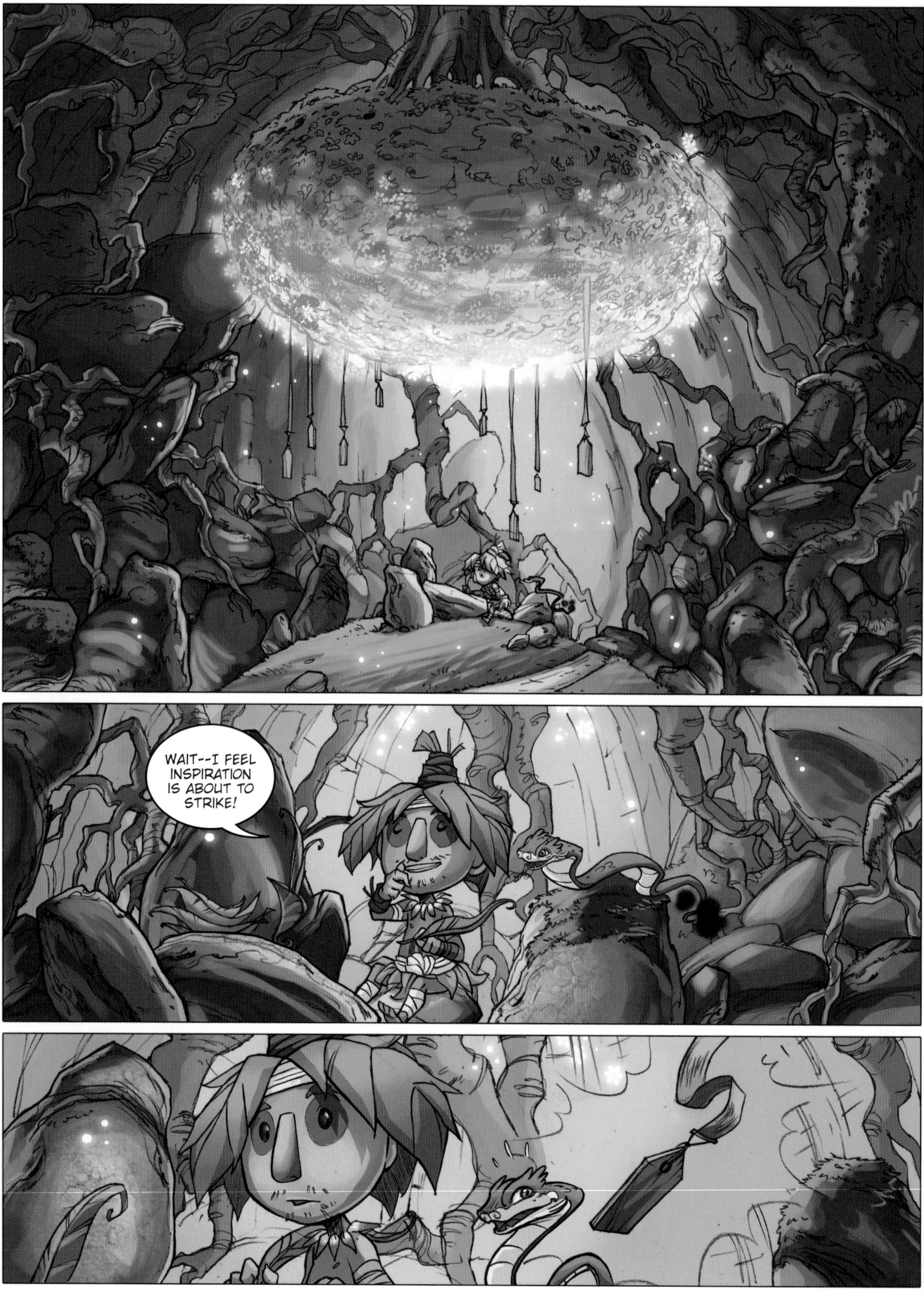
WAIT--I FEEL INSPIRATION IS ABOUT TO STRIKE!

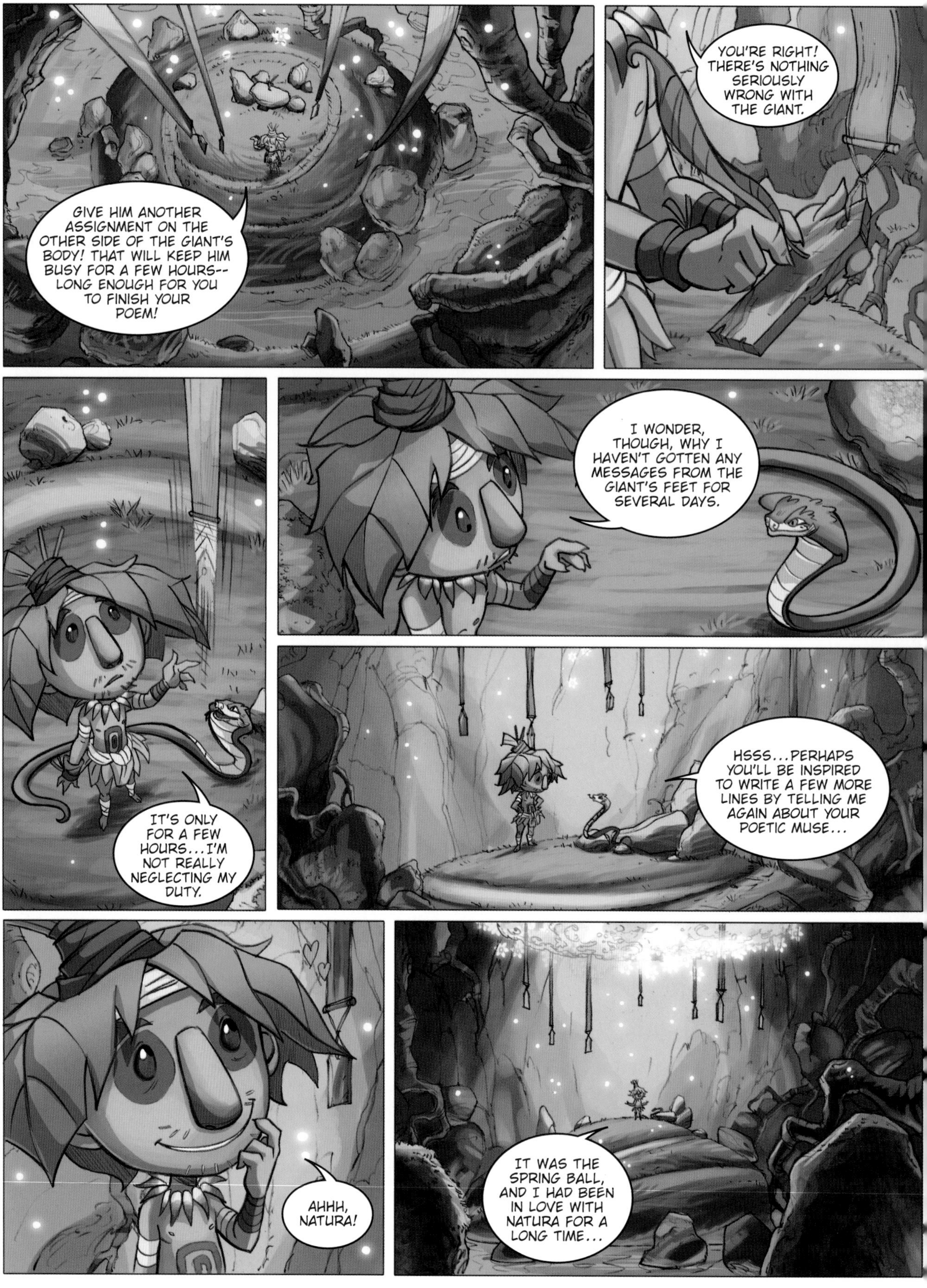

GIVE HIM ANOTHER ASSIGNMENT ON THE OTHER SIDE OF THE GIANT'S BODY! THAT WILL KEEP HIM BUSY FOR A FEW HOURS-- LONG ENOUGH FOR YOU TO FINISH YOUR POEM!
YOU'RE RIGHT! THERE'S NOTHING SERIOUSLY WRONG WITH THE GIANT.
IT'S ONLY FOR A FEW HOURS... I'M NOT REALLY NEGLECTING MY DUTY.
I WONDER, THOUGH, WHY I HAVEN'T GOTTEN ANY MESSAGES FROM THE GIANT'S FEET FOR SEVERAL DAYS.
HSSS... PERHAPS YOU'LL BE INSPIRED TO WRITE A FEW MORE LINES BY TELLING ME AGAIN ABOUT YOUR POETIC MUSE...
AHHH, NATURA!
IT WAS THE SPRING BALL, AND I HAD BEEN IN LOVE WITH NATURA FOR A LONG TIME...

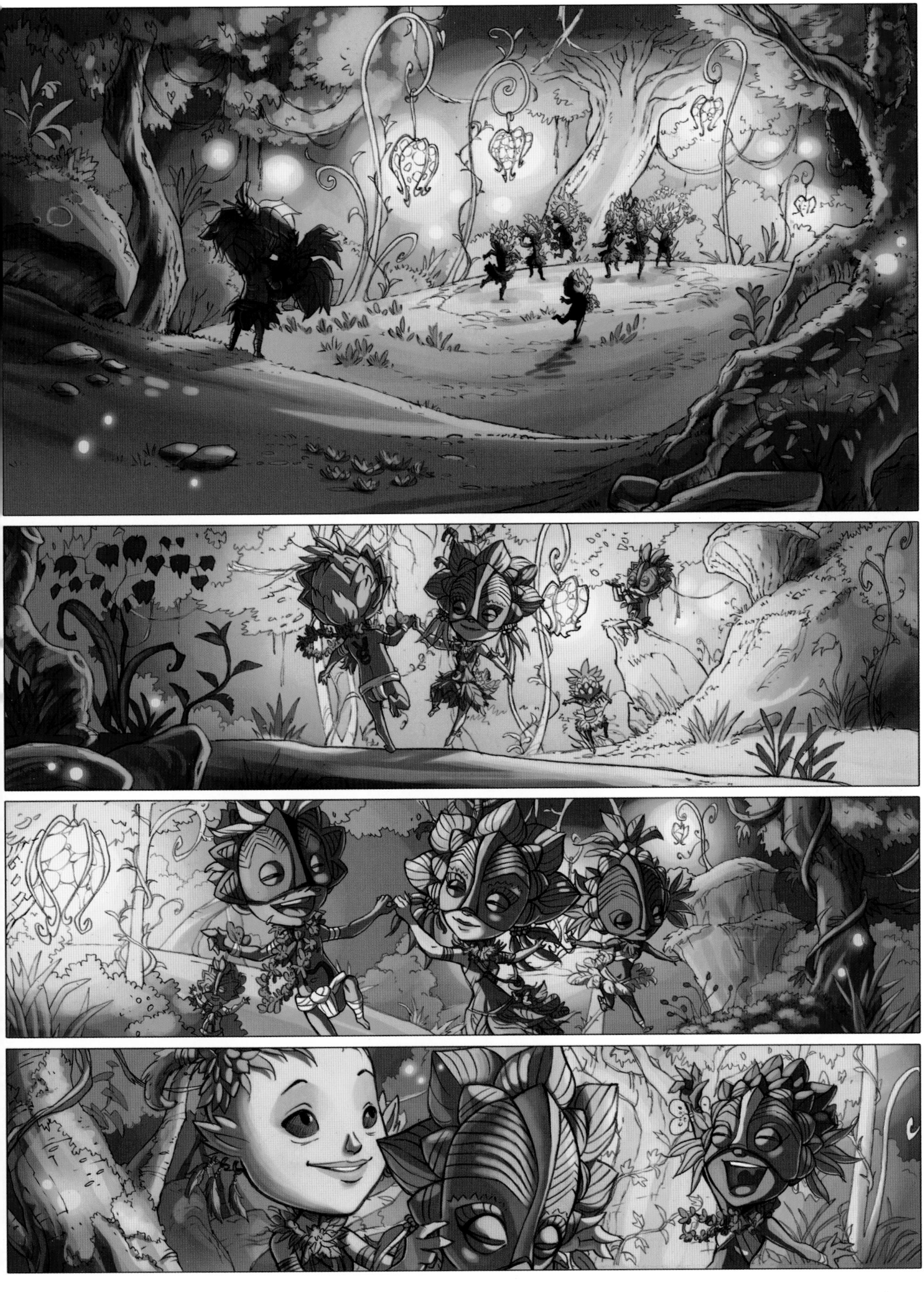

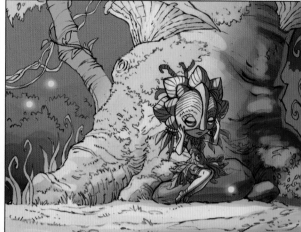

OH, NATURA, DAZZLING BEAUTY IN THE SUN'S PALE GLOW, MORE THAN THE STAR OF THE DAY, IT'S YOUR SPLENDOR THAT BLINDS ME.

OH, HOW PRETTY! BUT WHO...?

NATURA, FRAGRANT FLOWER, MAY OUR HANDS ENTWINE LIKE TENDRILS?

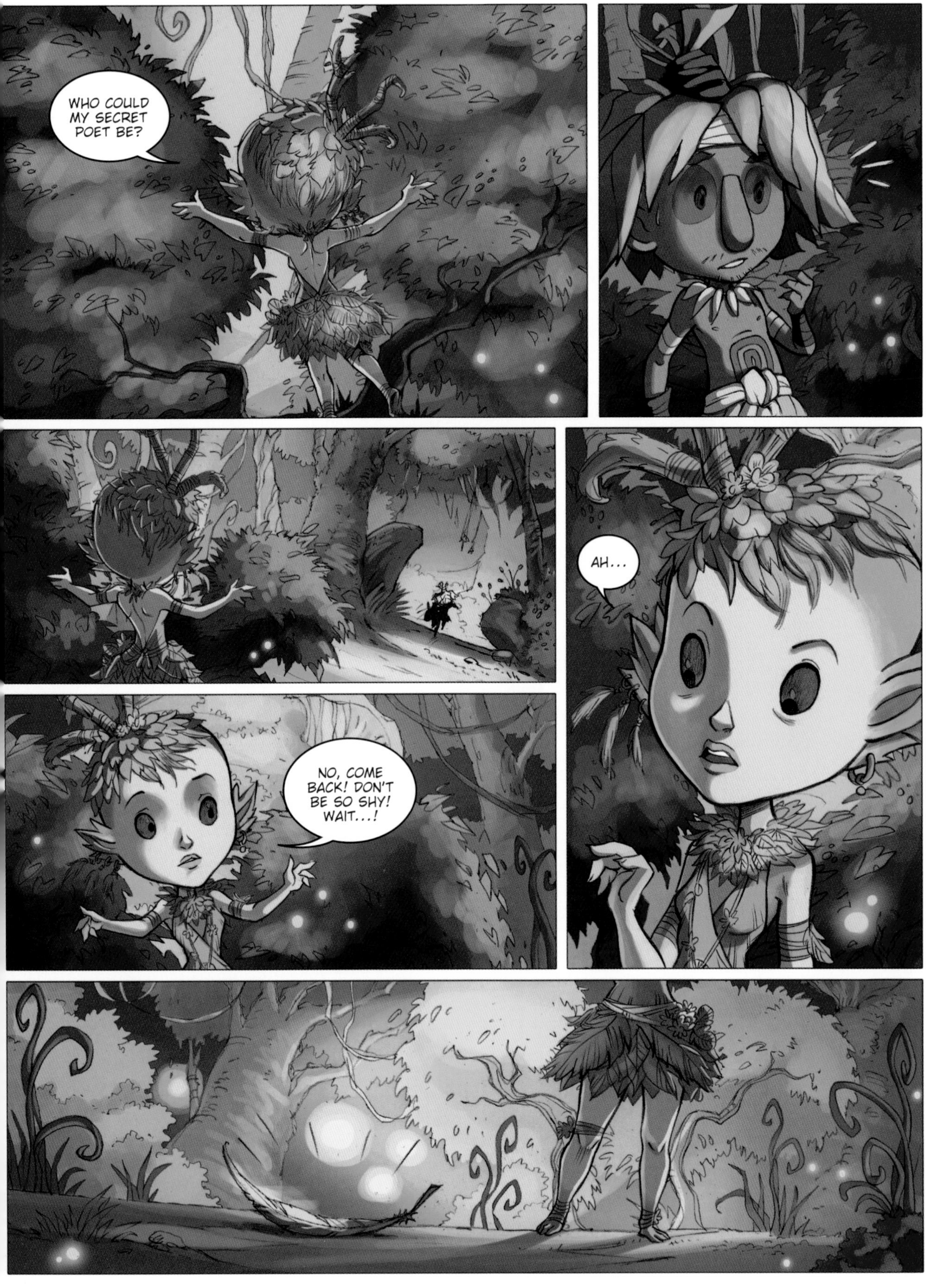

WHO COULD MY SECRET POET BE?
AH...
NO, COME BACK! DON'T BE SO SHY! WAIT...!

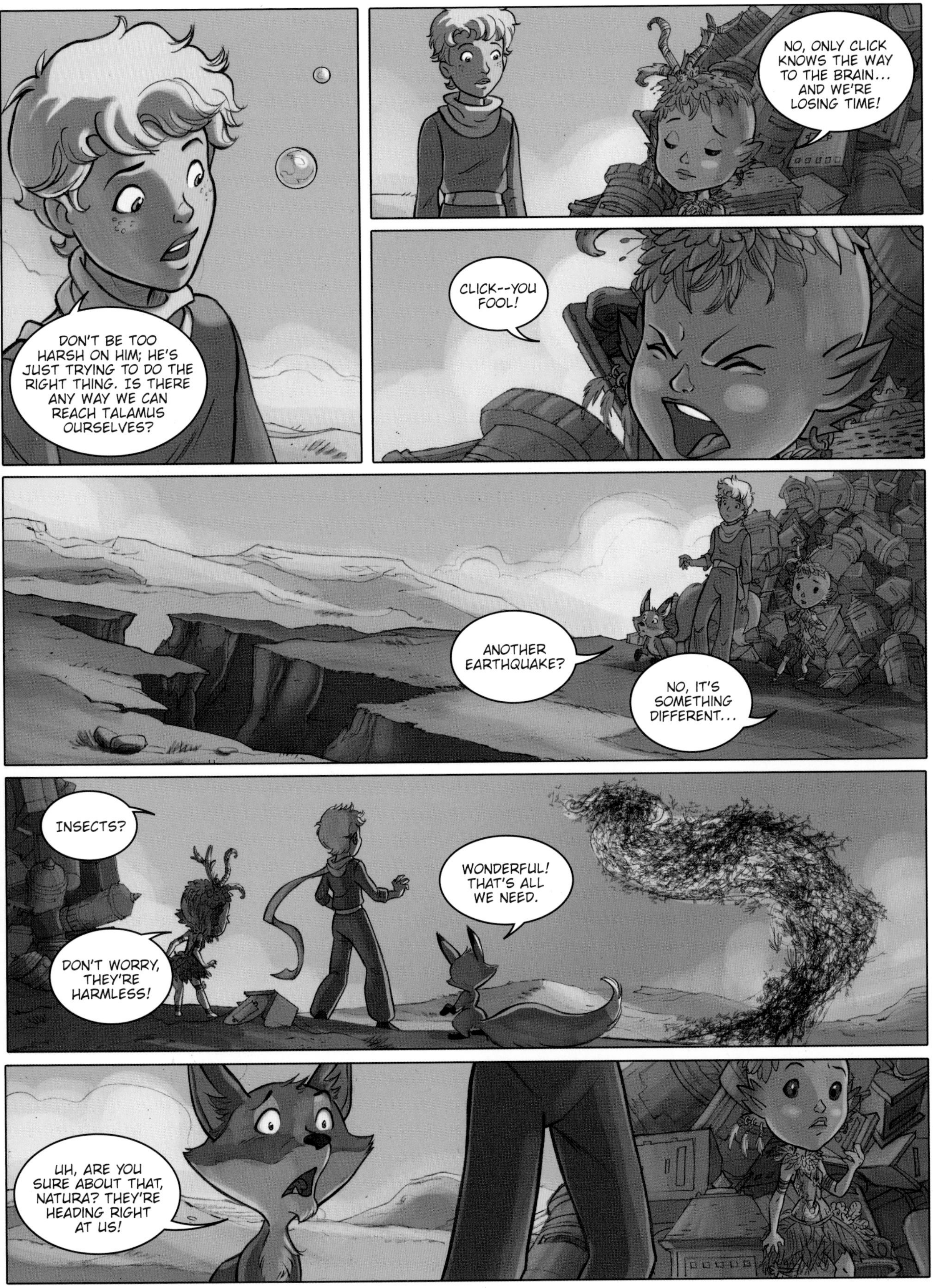
DON'T BE TOO HARSH ON HIM; HE'S JUST TRYING TO DO THE RIGHT THING. IS THERE ANY WAY WE CAN REACH TALAMUS OURSELVES?
NO, ONLY CLICK KNOWS THE WAY TO THE BRAIN... AND WE'RE LOSING TIME!
CLICK--YOU FOOL!
ANOTHER EARTHQUAKE?
NO, IT'S SOMETHING DIFFERENT...
INSECTS?
DON'T WORRY, THEY'RE HARMLESS!
WONDERFUL! THAT'S ALL WE NEED.
UH, ARE YOU SURE ABOUT THAT, NATURA? THEY'RE HEADING RIGHT AT US!

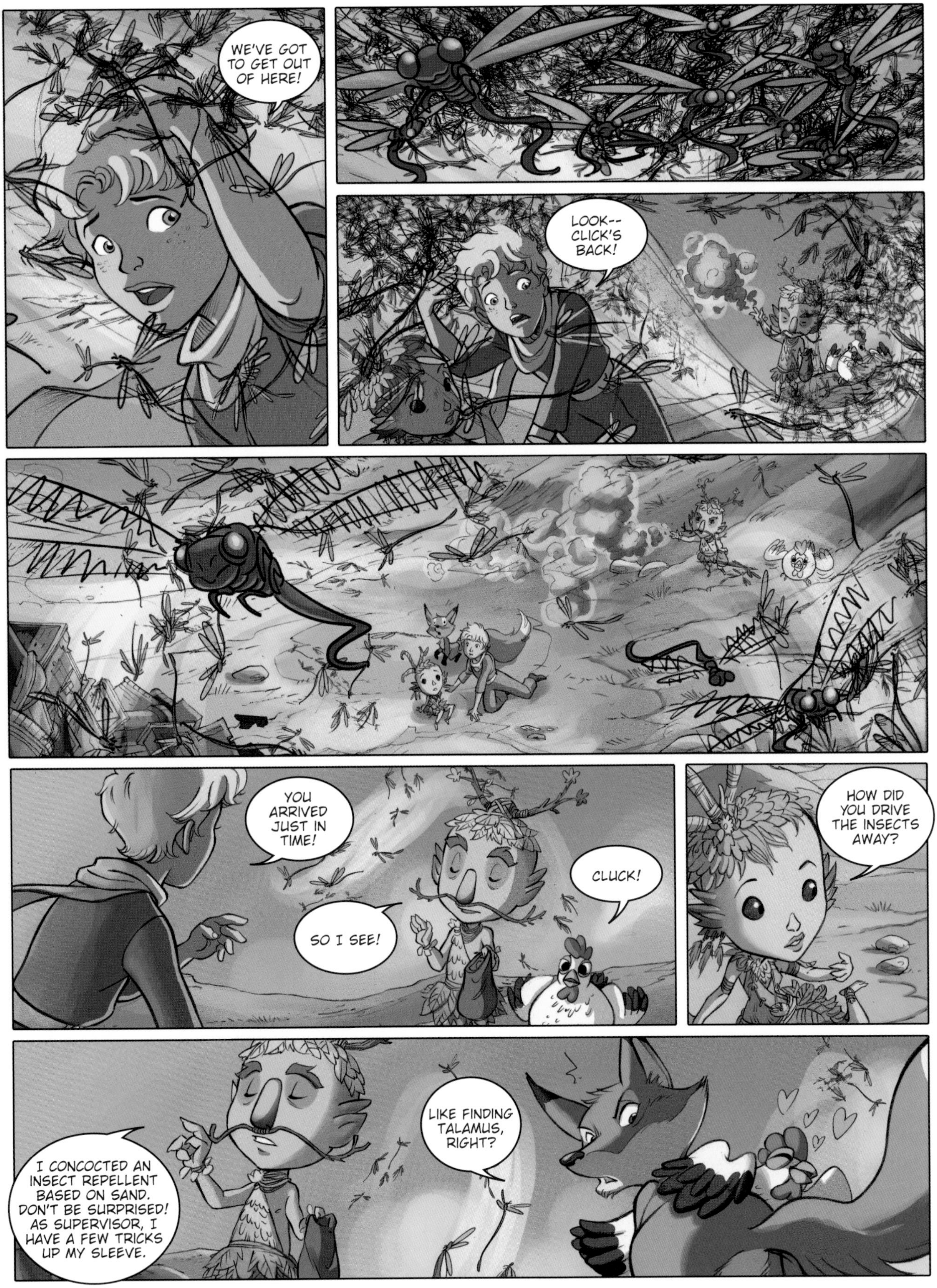
WE'VE GOT TO GET OUT OF HERE!
LOOK-- CLICK'S BACK!
YOU ARRIVED JUST IN TIME!
SO I SEE!
CLUCK!
HOW DID YOU DRIVE THE INSECTS AWAY?
I CONCOCTED AN INSECT REPELLENT BASED ON SAND. DON'T BE SURPRISED! AS SUPERVISOR, I HAVE A FEW TRICKS UP MY SLEEVE.
LIKE FINDING TALAMUS, RIGHT?

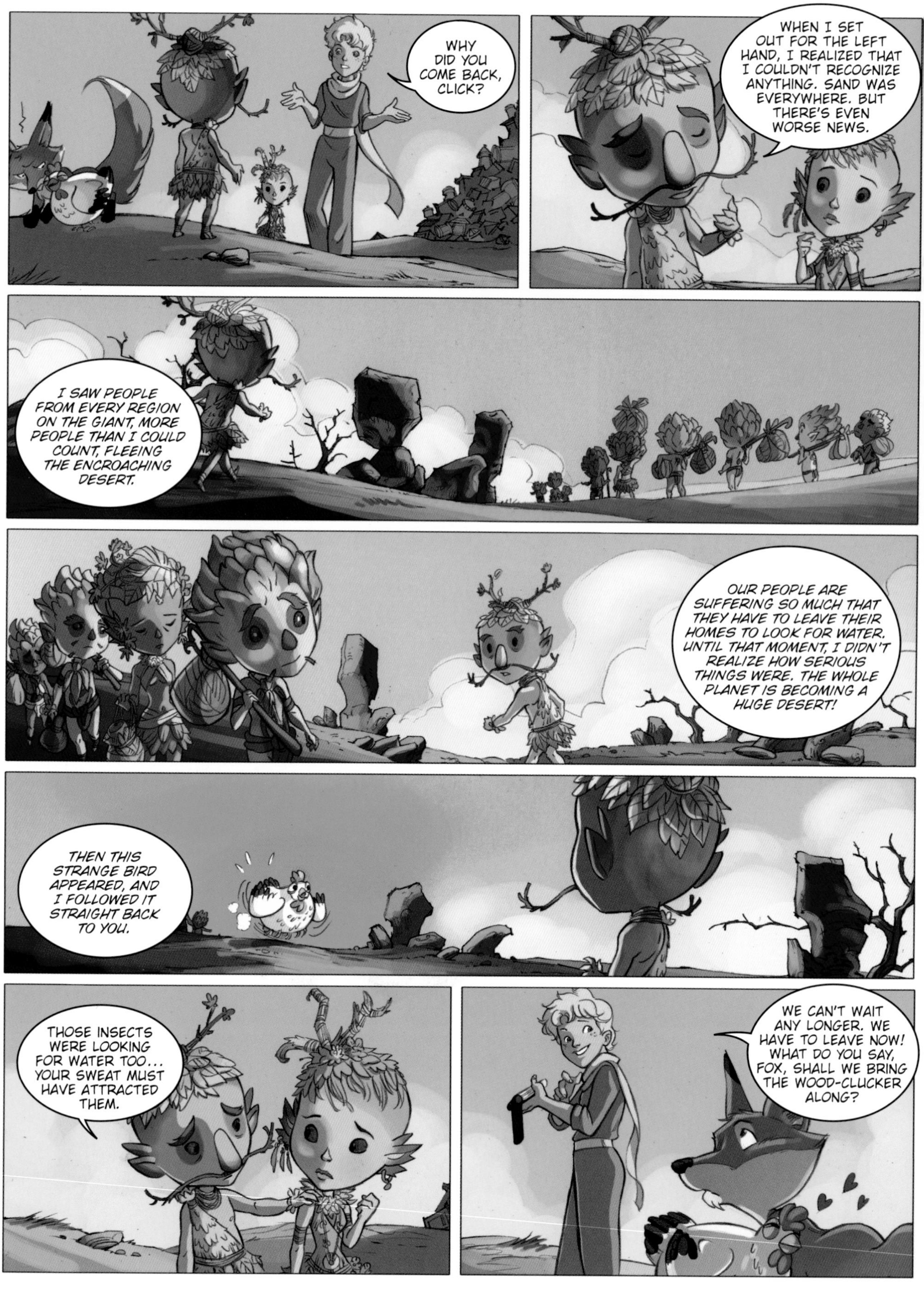
WHY DID YOU COME BACK, CLICK?
WHEN I SET OUT FOR THE LEFT HAND, I REALIZED THAT I COULDN'T RECOGNIZE ANYTHING. SAND WAS EVERYWHERE. BUT THERE'S EVEN WORSE NEWS.
I SAW PEOPLE FROM EVERY REGION ON THE GIANT, MORE PEOPLE THAN I COULD COUNT, FLEEING THE ENCROACHING DESERT.
OUR PEOPLE ARE SUFFERING SO MUCH THAT THEY HAVE TO LEAVE THEIR HOMES TO LOOK FOR WATER. UNTIL THAT MOMENT, I DIDN'T REALIZE HOW SERIOUS THINGS WERE. THE WHOLE PLANET IS BECOMING A HUGE DESERT!
THEN THIS STRANGE BIRD APPEARED, AND I FOLLOWED IT STRAIGHT BACK TO YOU.
THOSE INSECTS WERE LOOKING FOR WATER TOO... YOUR SWEAT MUST HAVE ATTRACTED THEM.
WE CAN'T WAIT ANY LONGER. WE HAVE TO LEAVE NOW! WHAT DO YOU SAY, FOX, SHALL WE BRING THE WOOD-CLUCKER ALONG?

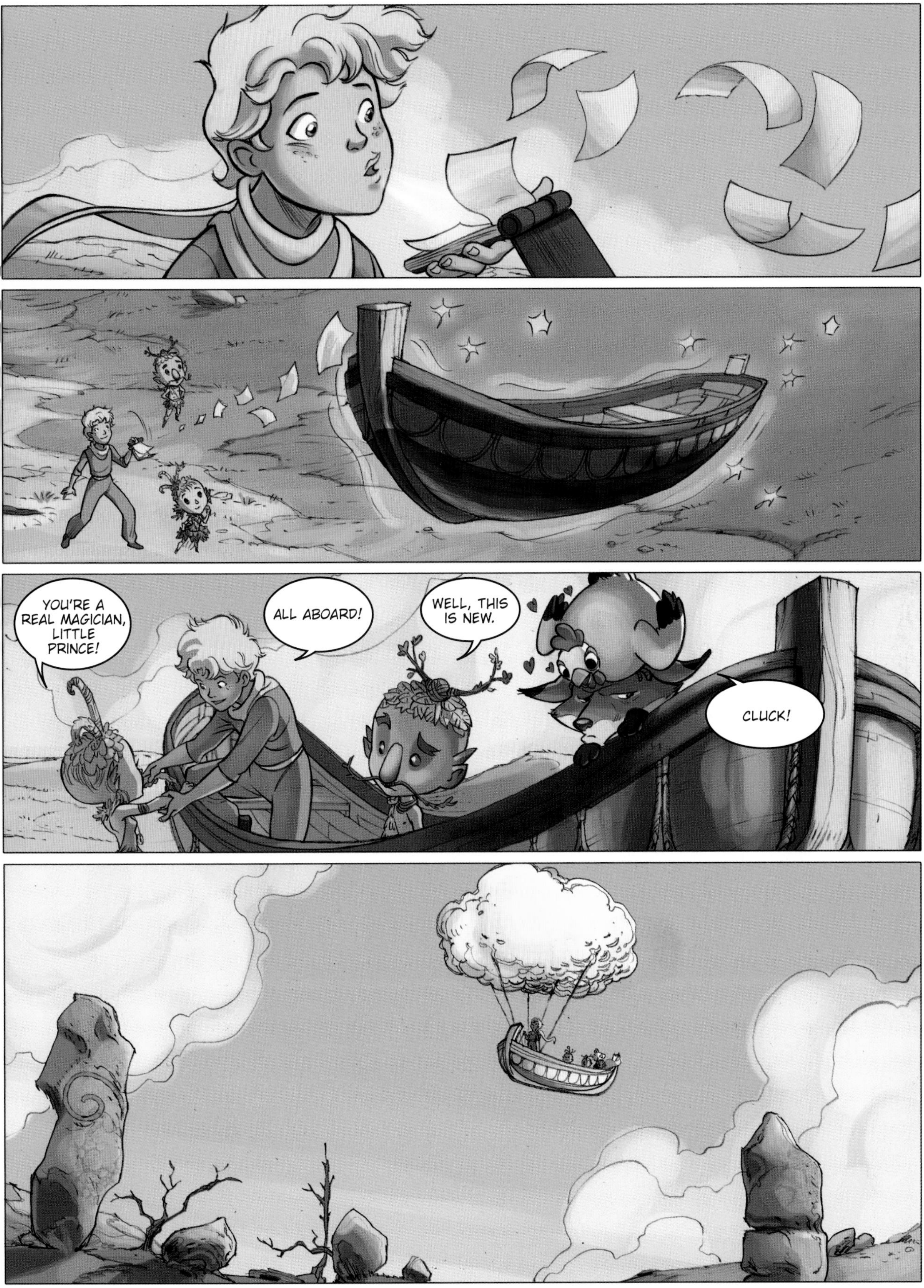
YOU'RE A REAL MAGICIAN, LITTLE PRINCE!
ALL ABOARD!
WELL, THIS IS NEW.
CLUCK!

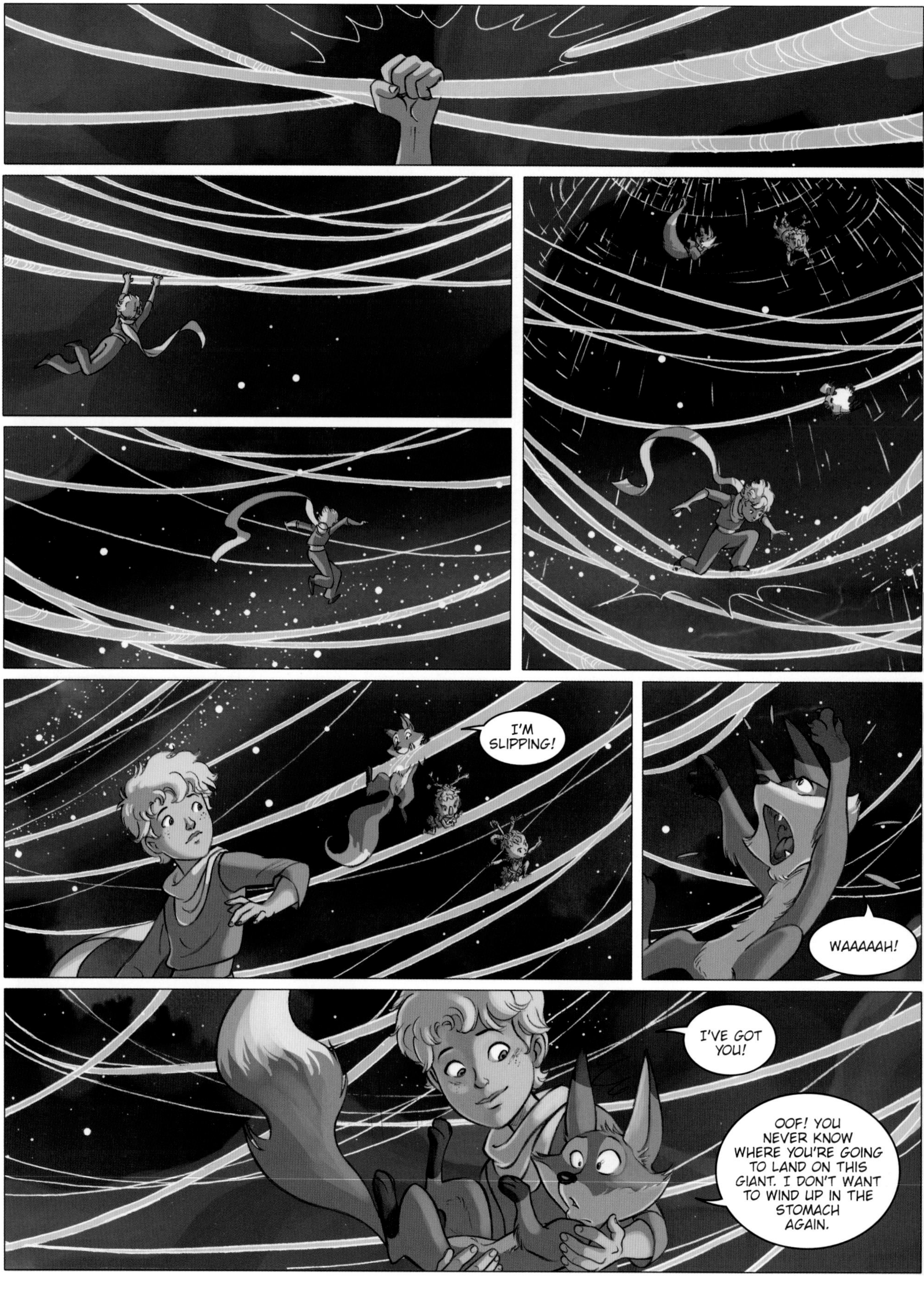
I'M SLIPPING!
WAAAAAH!
I'VE GOT YOU!
OOF! YOU NEVER KNOW WHERE YOU'RE GOING TO LAND ON THIS GIANT. I DON'T WANT TO WIND UP IN THE STOMACH AGAIN.

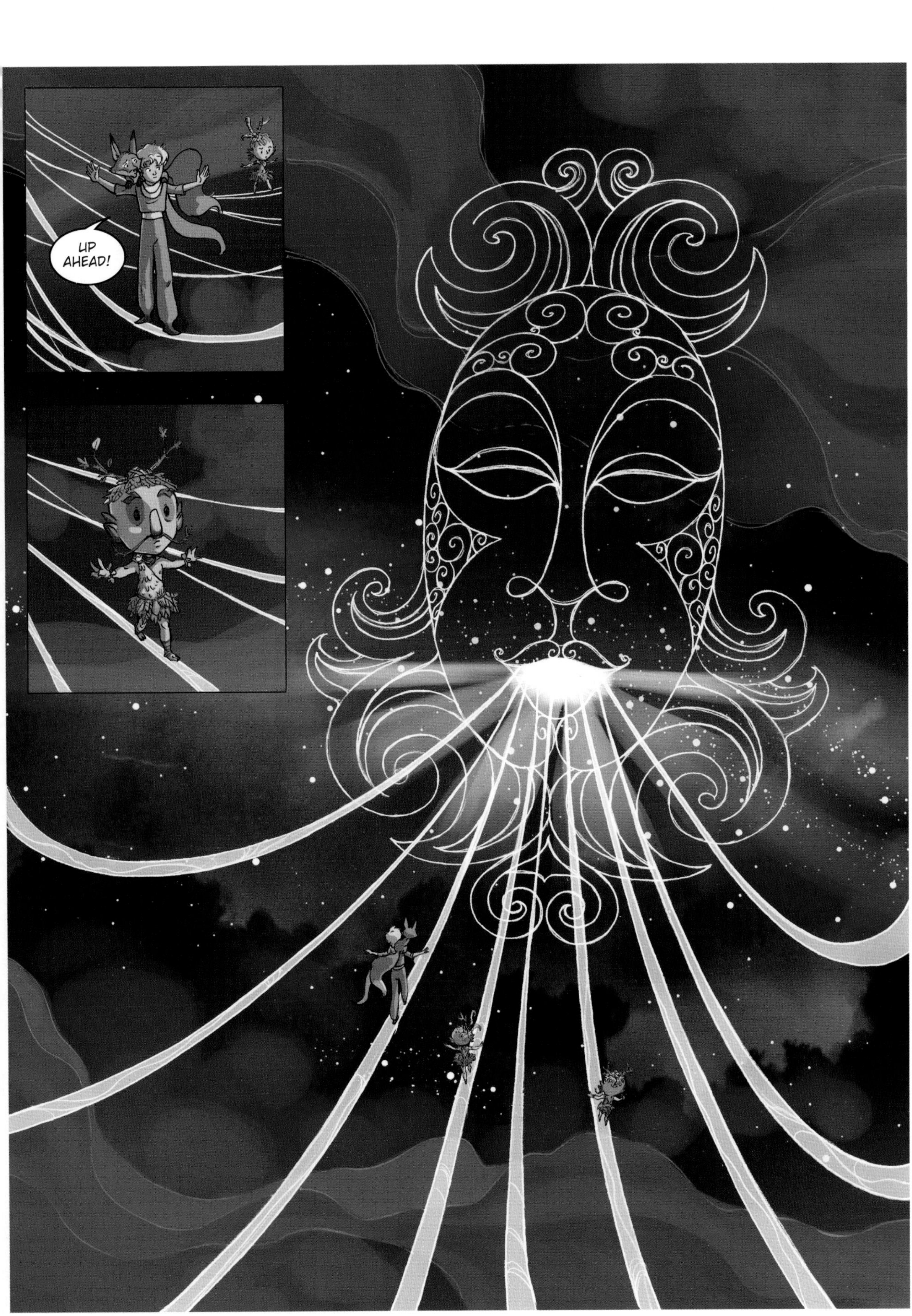
UP AHEAD!

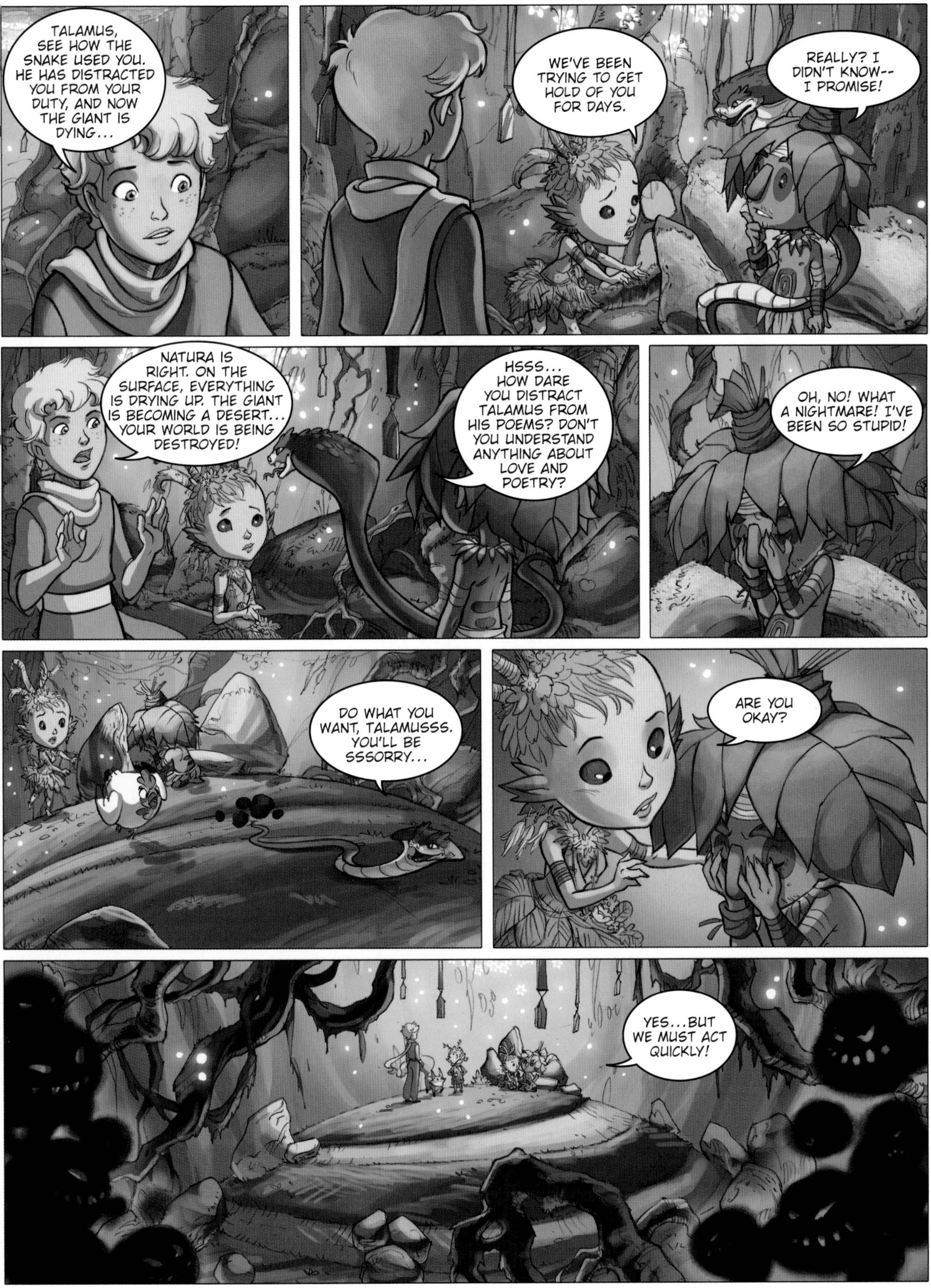
TALAMUS, SEE HOW THE SNAKE USED YOU. HE HAS DISTRACTED YOU FROM YOUR DUTY, AND NOW THE GIANT IS DYING...
WE'VE BEEN TRYING TO GET HOLD OF YOU FOR DAYS.
REALLY? I DIDN'T KNOW-- I PROMISE!
NATURA IS RIGHT. ON THE SURFACE, EVERYTHING IS DRYING UP. THE GIANT IS BECOMING A DESERT... YOUR WORLD IS BEING DESTROYED!
HSSS... HOW DARE YOU DISTRACT TALAMUS FROM HIS POEMS? DON'T YOU UNDERSTAND ANYTHING ABOUT LOVE AND POETRY?
OH, NO! WHAT A NIGHTMARE! I'VE BEEN SO STUPID!
DO WHAT YOU WANT, TALAMUSSS. YOU'LL BE SSSORRY...
ARE YOU OKAY?
YES...BUT WE MUST ACT QUICKLY!

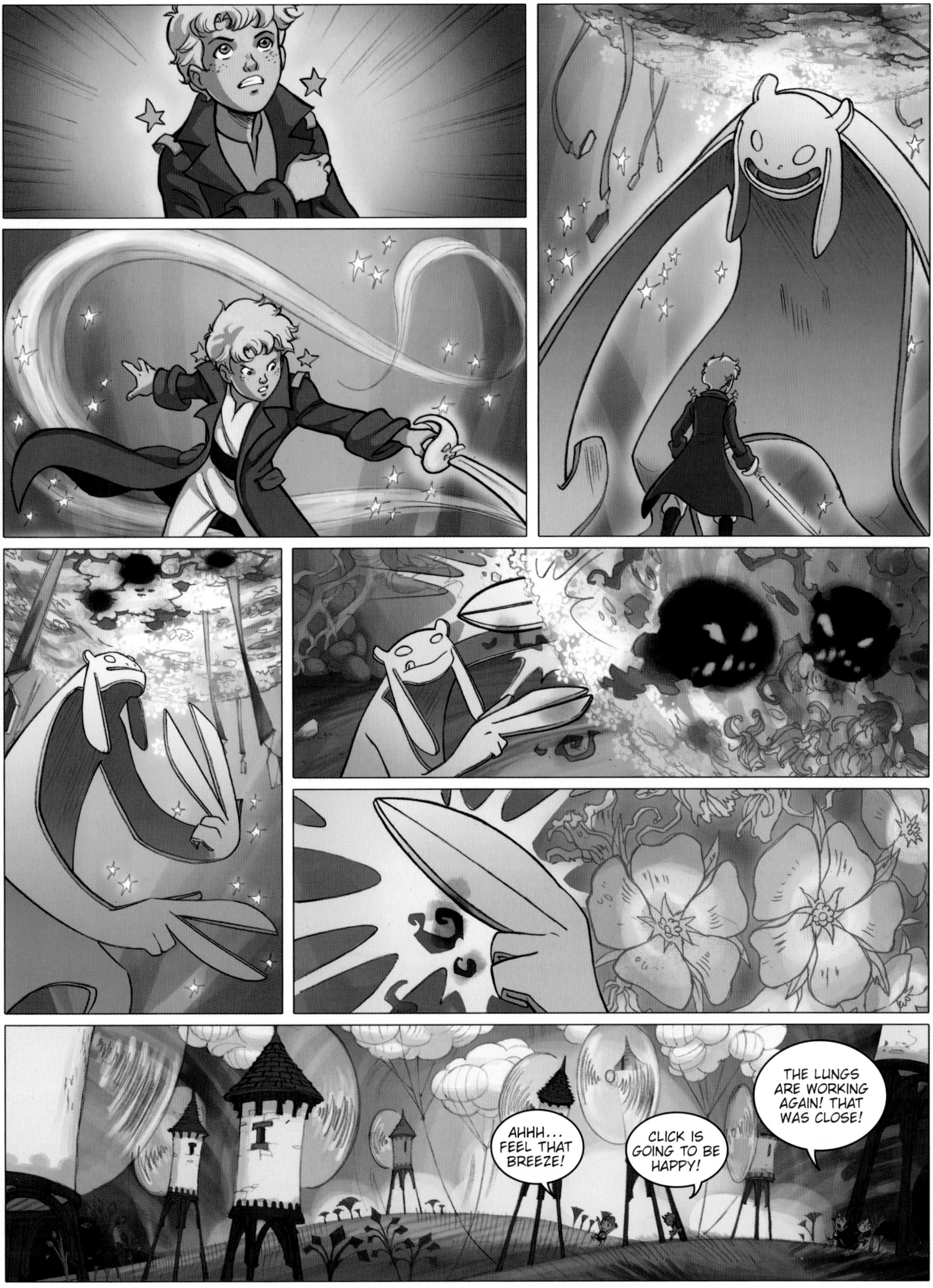
AHHH... FEEL THAT BREEZE!
CLICK IS GOING TO BE HAPPY!
THE LUNGS ARE WORKING AGAIN! THAT WAS CLOSE!

THE END

The Little Prince

AS IMAGINED BY
DIDIER CONVARD
&
PHILIPPE ADAMOV

COLORING
GREG SALSEDO

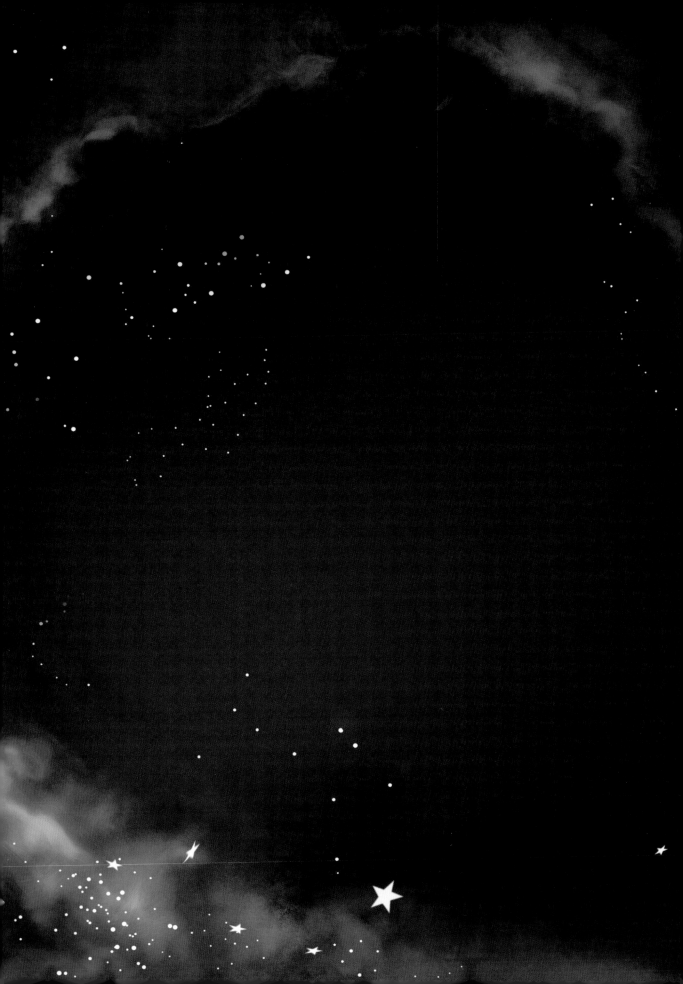

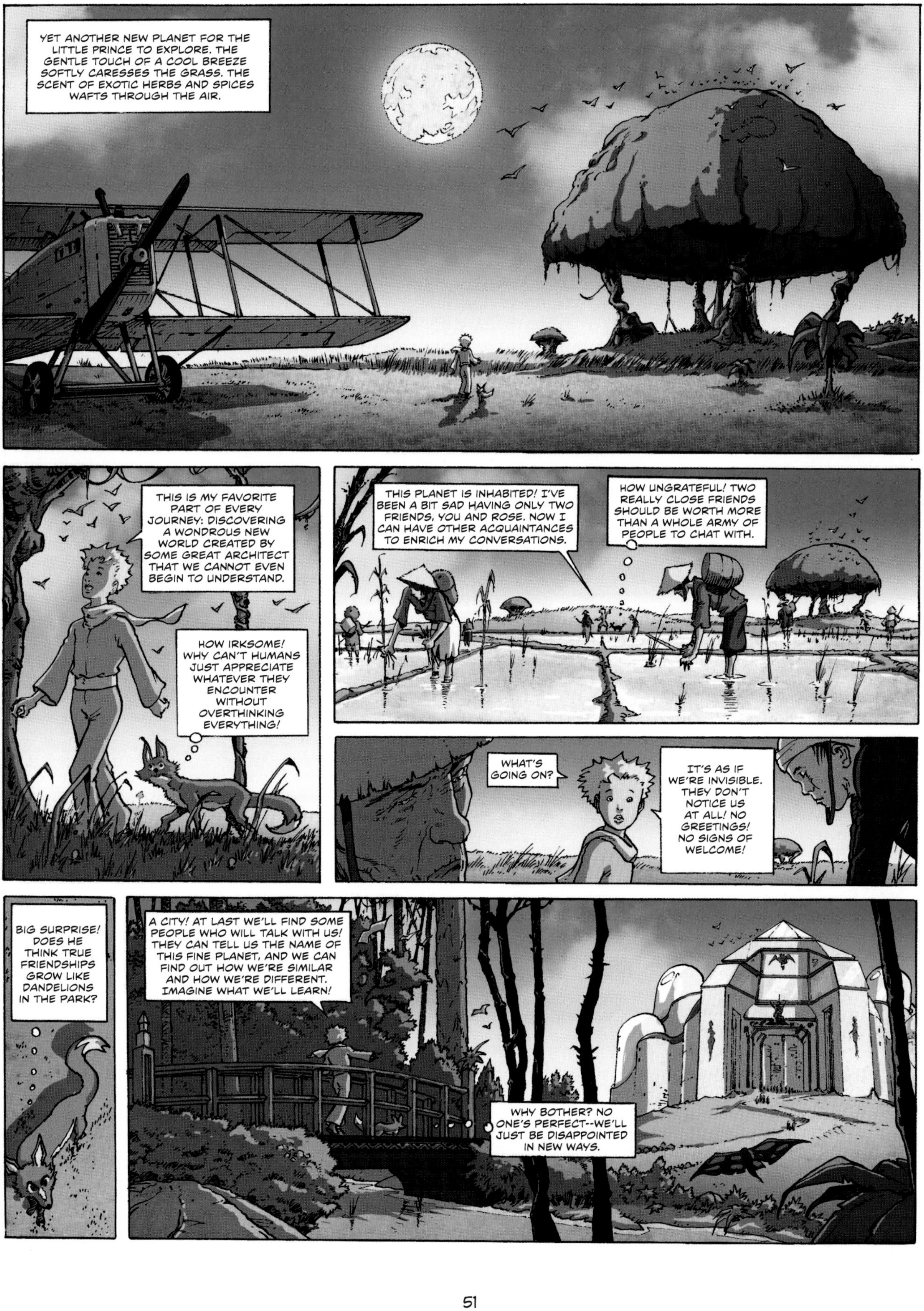
YET ANOTHER NEW PLANET FOR THE LITTLE PRINCE TO EXPLORE. THE GENTLE TOUCH OF A COOL BREEZE SOFTLY CARESSES THE GRASS. THE SCENT OF EXOTIC HERBS AND SPICES WAFTS THROUGH THE AIR.
THIS IS MY FAVORITE PART OF EVERY JOURNEY: DISCOVERING A WONDROUS NEW WORLD CREATED BY SOME GREAT ARCHITECT THAT WE CANNOT EVEN BEGIN TO UNDERSTAND.
HOW IRKSOME! WHY CAN'T HUMANS JUST APPRECIATE WHATEVER THEY ENCOUNTER WITHOUT OVERTHINKING EVERYTHING!
THIS PLANET IS INHABITED! I'VE BEEN A BIT SAD HAVING ONLY TWO FRIENDS, YOU AND ROSE. NOW I CAN HAVE OTHER ACQUAINTANCES TO ENRICH MY CONVERSATIONS.
HOW UNGRATEFUL! TWO REALLY CLOSE FRIENDS SHOULD BE WORTH MORE THAN A WHOLE ARMY OF PEOPLE TO CHAT WITH.
WHAT'S GOING ON?
IT'S AS IF WE'RE INVISIBLE. THEY DON'T NOTICE US AT ALL! NO GREETINGS! NO SIGNS OF WELCOME!
BIG SURPRISE! DOES HE THINK TRUE FRIENDSHIPS GROW LIKE DANDELIONS IN THE PARK?
A CITY! AT LAST WE'LL FIND SOME PEOPLE WHO WILL TALK WITH US! THEY CAN TELL US THE NAME OF THIS FINE PLANET, AND WE CAN FIND OUT HOW WE'RE SIMILAR AND HOW WE'RE DIFFERENT. IMAGINE WHAT WE'LL LEARN!
WHY BOTHER? NO ONE'S PERFECT--WE'LL JUST BE DISAPPOINTED IN NEW WAYS.

WHAT A FEAST FOR OUR SENSES! A KALEIDOSCOPE OF COLORS! INTOXICATING PERFUMES AND DELICATE FRAGRANCES! THE MURMUR OF A THOUSAND VOICES BLENDING INTO A MELODY AS CAPTIVATING AS THE SORCERER'S ENCHANTMENT!

HOW EASILY ENTERTAINED! HE'S LIKE A CHILD BEGUILED BY A PUPPET SHOW OR A NEW TYPE OF CANDY.

EXCUSE ME, WOULD YOU PLEASE TELL ME THE NAME OF THIS PLANET? MY FOX AND I ARE FROM ASTEROID B612, A SMALL PLANET NOT NEARLY AS IMPRESSIVE AS YOURS...

MIGHT I TROUBLE YOU FOR AN ANSWER TO MY QUESTION? WHAT KIND OF ADULTS ARE YOU? DON'T YOU REALIZE THAT IT'S COMMON COURTESY FOR ADULTS TO ANSWER A CHILD'S QUESTION?

WILL YOU LET ME JOIN YOUR GAME?

HOPE SPRINGS ETERNAL!

HOW DISAPPOINTING! NO DEFERENCE TO VISITING ROYALTY AT ALL!

I DON'T UNDERSTAND. NO ONE WILL PAY US THE SLIGHTEST ATTENTION!

WHAT A BLOW TO OUR SELF-ESTEEM!

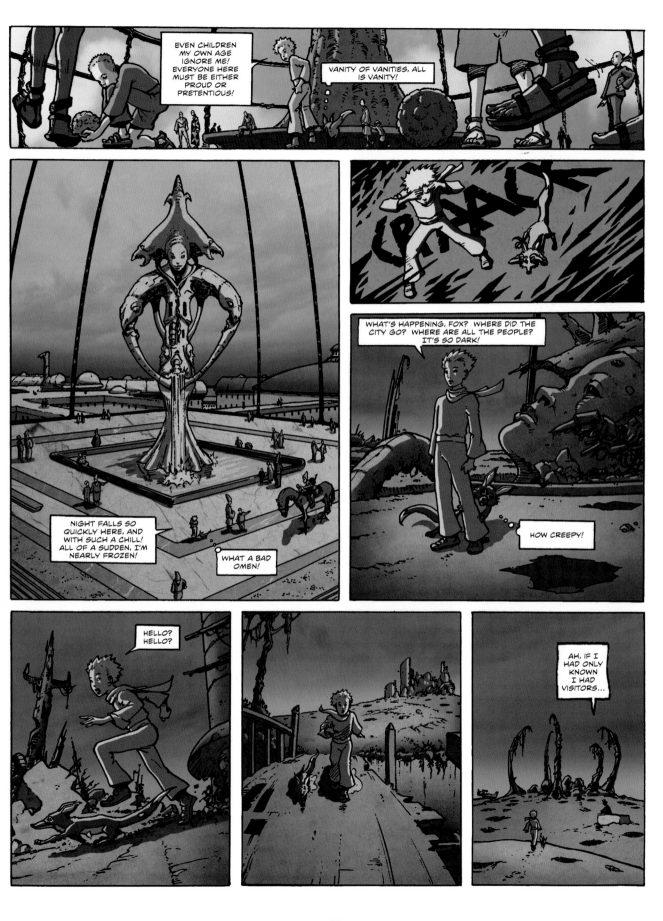

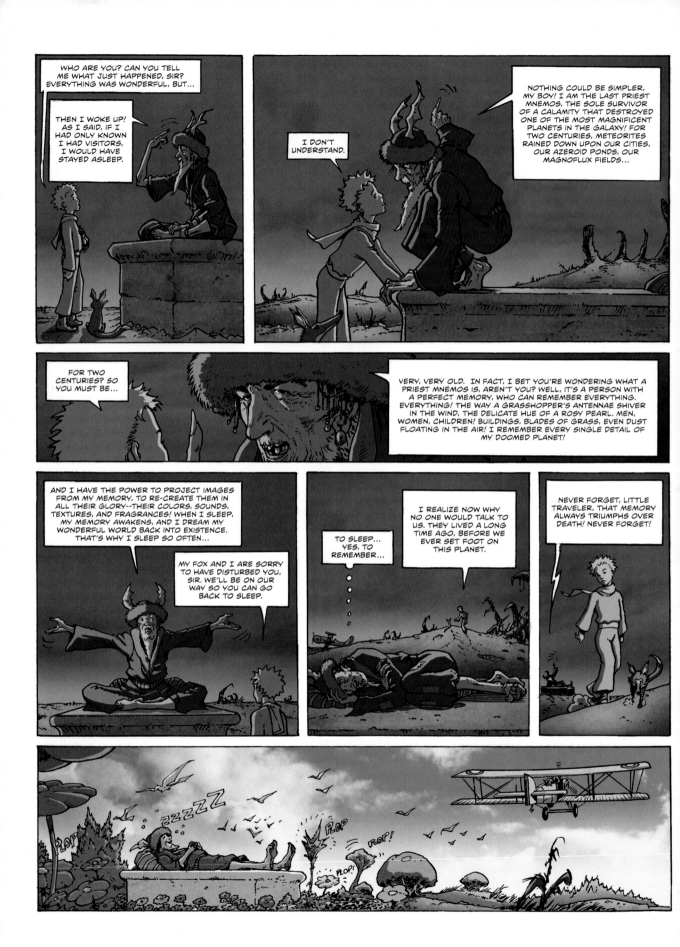

Antoine de Saint-Exupéry, author of the novel *The Little Prince* on which these new adventures are based, was born on June 29, 1900, in Lyon, France. He was the third of five children: Marie-Madeleine, Simone, Antoine, François, and Gabrielle. I was when he was twelve years old, during his summer break from boarding school that airplanes and flying first made a huge impression on him.

In 1920, he was accepted into the École des Beaux-Arts in Paris to study architecture, but the next year he joined the Second Aviation Regiment of the armed forces and received his pilot's license. In 1922, he had his first plane crash and suffered a head fracture. He had to leave the armed forces and work at different jobs on the ground to earn a living.

By May of 1926, Saint-Exupéry was able to fly again. He delivered airmail, which was a new and sometimes dangerous profession, on routes from France to Senegal and all the way to South America. That was where, in 1931, he met and married Consuelo Suncin.

From 1933 to 1938, Saint-Exupéry was very busy. He traveled to North Africa and Indochina and attempted to break the flight speed record from Paris to Saigon, Vietnam—during which his plane crashed again. It went down in the middle of the Sahara Desert. After his recovery, his life became even busier. He wrote newspaper reports in Spain on the Spanish Civil War, scouted airplane routes between Casablanca and Timbuktu, wrote a screenplay, registered several patents, and traveled to the United States. In 1939, with the start of World War II, he returned to France and talked his way into a job as a high-risk reconnaissance pilot for the French Air Force. But this only lasted until France reached an armistice agreement with Germany.

In December 1940, Saint-Exupéry returned to visit friends in New York, where he finally began work on *The Little Prince*. The story is narrated by a pilot who has crashed his plane into the Sahara Desert. He meets a little prince visiting from a faraway asteroid. Along the way, the prince also meets Fox and Snake. By late 1942, after spending the spring and summer writing and illustrating, Saint-Exupéry had completed his novel, and in April 1943 it was published in his native language of French *(Le Petit Prince)* and in English.

Saint-Exupéry was eager to return to the war. He decided to join the Free French Forces in Algeria, who were continuing the fight against the Axis powers. Because of his age, at first he had a hard time convincing them to let him fly. He was authorized to fly five dangerous missions. In fact, he flew eight. On July 31, 1944, Saint-Exupéry went on a scouting flight to prepare for military landings in the south of France. His plane disappeared over the water, and he was never seen again.

Over the decades since *The Little Prince* was published, it has gone on to become one of the best-selling novels of all time. In 2003, a small moon in our solar system's asteroid belt was named Petit-Prince in honor of the masterpiece Saint-Exupéry created.

THE LITTLE PRINCE IN THE TWENTY-FIRST CENTURY

The Little Prince is a landmark of literature and one of the most translated and beloved books in the world. It tackles universal topics with a unique philosophical and poetic sensibility. Sixty-five years after the first edition, the Saint-Exupéry Estate decided to bring the character back for a whole new generation . . . and for everyone who has ever loved the boy who sees the world with his heart.

The Little Prince now returns in a series of new adventures that remain true to the spirit of the original work. He will travel from planet to planet chasing the wicked Snake, who wants to plunge the whole universe into darkness. On each planet, the Snake sends bad thoughts into the minds of its inhabitants, making them sad and grim, draining the life out of their planet. The Little Prince must leave his beautiful Rose behind and must use his vision and courage to defeat the Snake, bringing along his friend Fox to save planets in danger across the universe.

ABOUT THE ADAPTERS

After several years in video games and Japanese animation, adapter Guillaume Dorison became literary editor for the publisher Les Humanoïdes Associés in 2006, where he launched the Shogun Collection dedicated to original manga. In June 2010, he founded Élyum Studio with Didier Poli, Jean-Baptiste Hostache, and Xavier Dorison to provide services for the creation of graphic novels. In addition to his position as director of writing for Élyum Studio, he has more than two dozen comics and manga to his credit under the pseudonym IZU, has written several titles in the Explora series on world explorers for French publisher Glénat, and won the 2010 Animeland Prize for best French manga.

Didier Poli, artistic director for the new graphic novel adaptations based on *The Little Prince*, was born in Lyon in 1971. After graduate studies in applied arts, he worked for various animation studios including Disney. He was working as artistic director for the video game company Kalisto Entertainment when he met Manuel Bichebois in 2001 and began drawing Bichebois's graphic novel series L'Enfant de l'orage. At the 2004 Nîmes Festival, Didier Poli received the Bronze Boar prize for young talent. He continues, along with his work on graphic novels, to work regularly in cartoons and video games as a designer and storyboard artist.

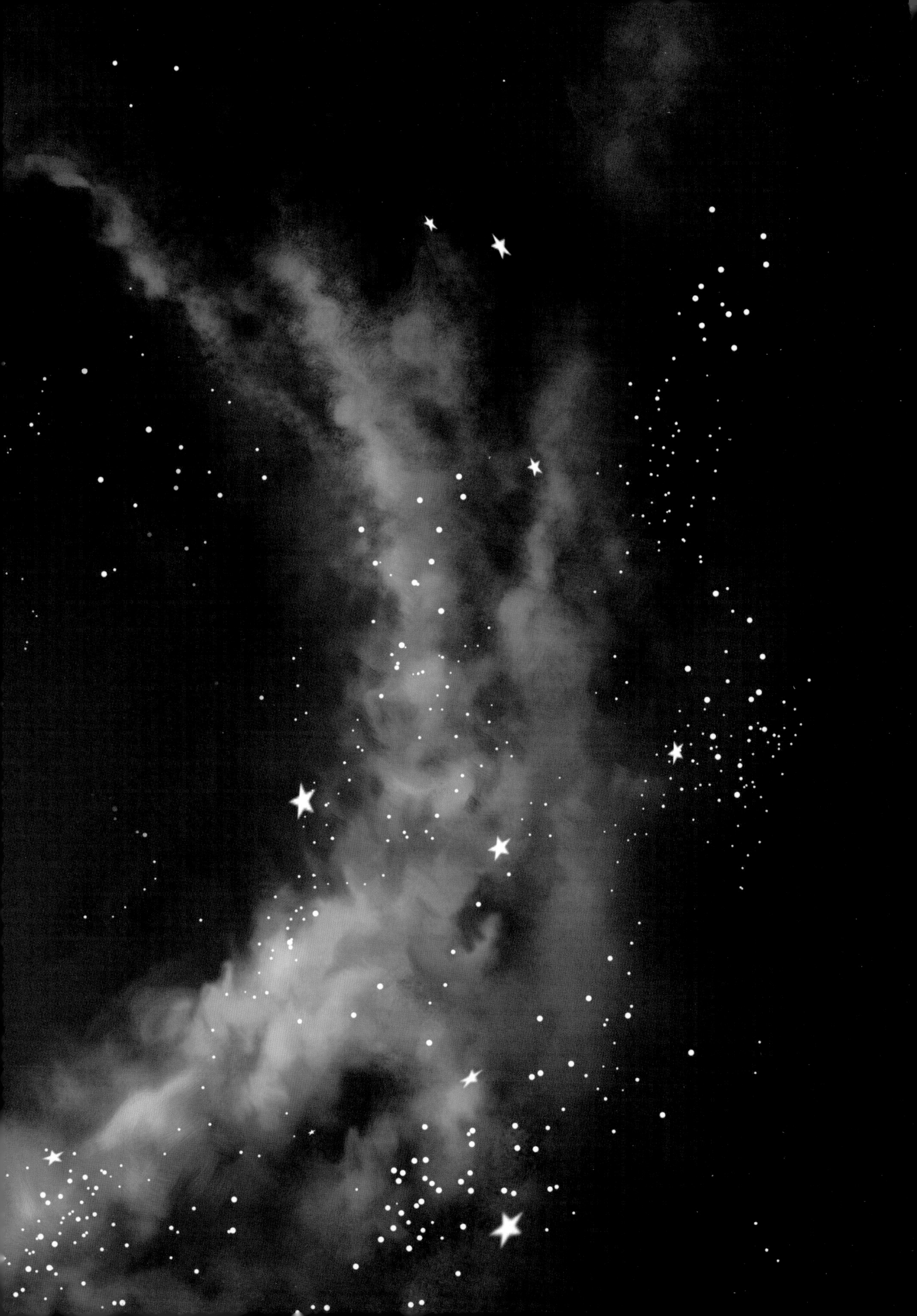